The golden body lay with ... with the earth and the roc... silver down covered it: unconscious, unmoving ... ribs and belly gave with breathing.

And female. Merritt approached it carefully, not least for the hazard of the slide ... a woman-sized, fragile shape, long-limbed. He bent and gingerly touched the long-fingered hand that was so nearly and so much not — human. The face was humanlike: long eyes, closed, with silver lashes and faint silver brows; a short, flat nose; a thin, wide mouth — prognathic features, jaw farther forward then human, but delicate. Merritt considered a moment, reluctant to take that alien thing into his arms, next his throat. Finally, with great tenderness of her injuries, he lifted her to him and rose.

"I'd never seen one," said Jim, at his shoulder, and a flush came to his young face. "Sam, she's just about human, isn't she?"

"Just about." Merritt hesitated — chilled to the depth of him ...

Also by C. J. Cherryh in VGSF

ANGEL WITH THE SWORD

THE DREAMSTONE

THE TREE OF SWORDS AND JEWELS

C. J. CHERRYH

Hestia

VGSF

VGSF is an imprint of Victor Gollancz Ltd
14 Henrietta Street, London WC2E 8QJ

First published in Great Britain 1988
by Victor Gollancz Ltd

First VGSF edition 1988

Copyright © 1979 by C. J. Cherryh

British Library Cataloguing in Publication Data
Cherryh, C. J.
　Hestia.
　I. Title
　813'.54[F]　　PR3553.H358

ISBN 0-575-04042-4

Printed and bound in Great Britain
by Richard Clay Ltd, Bungay, Suffolk

Hestia

1

The shuttle was visible through the rain-spattered glass, an alien shape in New Hope, towering sleek and silver among brown, unpainted buildings. It rested here only briefly: *Adam Jones* was in orbit about the world, a few days' interlude in her star-to-star voyaging, and the shuttle belonged to her, and to another existence, an alien dream in Hestia's sole brown-hued city.

Rain was the prime reality on Hestia: mist hazed distances and blurred the edges of middle-ground objects; rain pooled in the muddy streets and dripped and sweated from decaying buildings; gray monotones of cloud and brown of earth and flood persisted, while the colony died.

In the streets a thin shout went up. A group of revelers snaked by, arms linked, weaving and slipping in the mud, ignoring the drizzle. It was festival; a ship was in port. They paused, lifted a bottle in drunken salute, shouted something and wove away, linked, drab brown-clad folk quickly lost in the rain-haze and the maze of their ramshackle buildings.

Sam Merritt let the homespun curtain fall across the depressing sight and paced back to his chair, where papers were scattered on the scarred table. This unpainted room with the creaking wooden flooring was all that Hestia afforded of governmental splendor, New Hope's official residence, its best hospitality; and Merritt cast a regretful glance at his baggage still sitting unpacked, a forlorn cluster of black cases in the center of the floor.

A door opened and banged shut downstairs; footsteps creaked heavily up the treads. Merritt let himself down onto the hard chair by the table and leaned against the edge, gave a casual glance as the door opened and Don Hathaway slouched in, rain-damp and grim. Hathaway brushed droplets from his jacket and wiped his hair back, sank down on a corner of the nearer bed, shoulders sagging. He was older than Merritt's twenty-eight years, gray-templed. His face was growing heavy and habitually sullen, and the lines had been deepened since their landing.

"Been out in the town," Hathaway said.

Merritt nodded. That bleak look did not invite comment.

"Sam," Hathaway said, "when we touched down and had a look about, I kept telling myself it had to be better somewhere . . . in town, out-country, somewhere. But the governor's briefing this morning—" He gestured loosely at the table, the scattered papers. "It's finished, Sam."

"What do you mean?"

"I talked to Al a few minutes ago, out in the town. And when that shuttle lifts, we're going to be on her."

Merritt looked at him, swallowed, shook his head: no refusal, but an echo of Hathaway's despair. His

8

heart was beating hard. "Seven years of traveling to get here, Don—for turning around again—"

"And maybe we'll live to see home again." Hathaway wiped at his graying hair and rose, walked to the bedside table where a bottle sat, gathered up the dirty glasses with it and brought them to the big table, set them down and poured. He sat down then and pushed one across to Merritt. "Been out in the town. Seen it. Seen enough, Sam. Mud and farmers and things falling apart. And the mentality of these people—look at this place. Falling down, and not a hand turned to clean it, let alone fix it. Saw a man sitting out there in the rain, just sitting, drunk and staring at the water. Saw machinery patched with wooden parts, to work by hand. Windows patched with wood and paper. A boy tried to knife one of the crew last night, did you hear that?"

"Drunk, probably."

"Tried to rob him."

"These people begged for help fifty years ago, Don. They're destitute. Is it their fault?"

"Well, it's no fault of ours, either. We don't have to spend a year of our lives paying for it."

"The government is paying us plenty. Think of that. Add that up, what it'll mean to us."

"The agreement said—" Hathaway jabbed a finger at his palm "—that we were to come out here and look over the situation first-hand, to see if we could work out a system to control the floods . . . or to see if the world has the resources left to handle the problem at all. *If it has the resources left*. I've made my determination on that score. If you agree and go along—"

"Pull out without even looking at the upper valley? Don, we owe them at least that much."

"The ship's calling the shuttle up and she won't wait. You know what's involved, to throw a starship off-schedule."

"So for the sake of a year's wait on the next ship, you're going to throw this colony and a good slice of our own lives—"

"Sam, Sam, if I thought it would do any possible good, I'd go up there and look at that valley till the sun froze. But listen: listen to me. Even the original survey said this valley wasn't right for permanent settlement. And what did these people do? They ignored that instruction and built homes here. It's their own stupid choice. Another point: equipment. It's beyond recovery, flooded out, lost, cannibalized, broken, whatever. Our contract runs five years on-world at most. What could we do here in that time? Nothing. Nothing that could make any difference. They'd be needing other engineers to replace us and that could take decades, while all we've done goes sliding into the mud and bureaucrats dawdle. Hestia isn't going to live through another long wait. No. Someone's got to make the decision and get these people off this world or out of that valley, and that's not our field. I say we recommend removal, emergency basis, and leave nothing in the hands of the bureaucrats. So we take our million for riding out here to look; and we split it and go to the next prosperous world and retire. It's best, even for the Hestians. No need to be ashamed of that. It's crueler the other way."

Merritt shook his head, looked at the room, at

Hathaway. "They'll not go easy. A year, one year . . . just the effort, even a useless one . . . don't you think they'd accept the decision to abandon the colony a lot more readily if they knew we'd seen the situation ourselves, if they knew we'd tried?"

"Sam, I'm forty years old. By the time I get somewhere else I'll be closer to fifty. I came out here maybe to settle down and practice my profession; but it's hopeless. There's nothing here. I'm getting out of this now, while it's quiet, before these drunken farmers have the chance to realize what the score is. Selfish—maybe. But so far as I'm concerned I've fulfilled that contract and I've nothing to be ashamed of. I came, where most wouldn't; and I took the chance and I've seen what I want to see, and all I want to see, ever. I'm not going to waste the rest of my life on this."

"Does Al . . ." Merritt asked finally, "does Al feel the same way?"

"Yes. Look, you'll get somewhere worth living for when you're thirty-six, thirty-seven, something like that. You'll have time to start over and enjoy that half million. Right now maybe you've got leisure for mistakes, or think you have. Don't think I don't understand how you feel. I was seven years younger when I started out on this crazy project—but seven years more will change your perspective plenty. You owe yourself better than Hestia has to give."

"Give it a year."

Hathaway frowned and looked at the floor and up again. "I've been too long on *Adam Jones* to want to change ships for so little advantage to anyone. All right, I'll admit it: I want the comfort of people I know around me. I want my friends. I want the place I'm used to. I gave Hestia most of my young life. I'm not going to throw the rest of it away on a lost cause. I'm going out on the ship that brought us."

"Isn't it maybe something you decided ... even before you saw the world?"

"Sam—I resent that."

"Isn't it the truth, after all? Now you've talked Al into agreeing with you. You'll get him to sign that removal, and all you need is me."

"Look, every year we put these people off with false hopes more of them are going to die in the long run. That's no kindness. You know if we don't stay, if we've left a marker aloft with that order, these folk will be taken out with the next ship; and that's the best thing we could do for them."

"The colonists won't go. They'll fight at having it done this way. They've proven that. *Adam Jones* tried to take them off once before; other ships have likely tried. They won't. You and Al and I, we could prove to them it's best."

"We can prove it by leaving. They'll fold, when they're facing reality, when they have to realize there's going to be no help from Earth. And so what if they're willing to fight over the question? Does that give us equipment or help us stop the rain?"

"It's not right."

"It's not as if the whole colonial program depended on Hestia any longer. They—"

"Aren't important."

"Sam, they were supposed to have gone from phase one to industry fifty years ago, but they're going steadily downhill. They're without machines or

12

power. Most of the last generation hasn't learned to read."

"So we take them off Hestia and drop them into a culture they can't hope to understand."

"Or let them starve here. Sam, they knew, they knew this was coming. They knew from the start the valley would flood whenever the weather rolled around to one of its long wet cycles; they were to use the valley and then move out of it; but no, they didn't believe geosurvey; they've been sitting here a hundred years absorbing what they were given in the way of aid; and now they want us to build them their dams so they can go on sitting and vegetating."

"The floods got them before they had a chance. What could they do once they'd lost their machines and their momentum? They've survived. They've done that for themselves."

"Don't tell me they've tried. Look at New Hope. This rotting mansion is the only building in all the town that was really built as a residence, and it was the old colony dormitory. The rest of the buildings were all warehouses—or are to this day; and not a building in the whole town is younger than a hundred years. They haven't touched this place, they haven't done anything or built anything together since the day they were founded. They chose their little plots of land upriver, gave up any concern for government or for the colony's future. They just let all cooperative projects go until it was just too late. They don't even have electricity, for pity's sake. Now the farmland's gone, silted into the bay so they can't use that either; and they're breeding insects and disease out there in the summers in that lagoon. They die of diseases nowhere else has heard of. *Adam Jones* will put us all through decontamination or risk carrying plague from here to Pele."

"With drainage, dams, power production—"

"Ah, Sam, they'll do that when they fly unaided. No. I've ordered my baggage back to the ship and so has Al. Want yours moved with it—or do you want to go it alone?"

Merritt stared elsewhere, at the windows, at the steady drip of rain. Thin shouts drifted up from outside.

"That's how it is," said Hathaway. "If you won't sign the removal, it won't go through; we'll lose the money. Al—gets his. His contract is prepaid. All you can do is hold me from mine. From any future. From all I have left. You want to do that?"

Merritt shook his head. "If you and Al are going, there's no arguing, is there? If you'll go without the money—there's no way. All right. I'll sign your paper."

"Crew's going to assist. They'll carry in some mean-ingless crates, get our luggage out again. When people here find out—"

The downstairs door opened and closed. Hathaway put himself on his feet. Merritt did likewise, went to the window and looked out anxiously; there was no one. Single footsteps sounded on the board stairs, light and quick, and reached the door.

It opened. Lilith Courtenay slipped inside with a lithe move and shut it quickly—silver-suited and glistening with rain, a glimpse of elsewhere in the drab room. She shook back her hood, looked about with a grimace and a look of disbelief. *Adam Jones* was stitched on her sleeve, and the emblems of worlds and stars years removed from Hestia: crew, and disdainful of the worlds the patches signified, a breed apart from groundlings.

"I wouldn't have expected *you*." Merritt. said. His pulse was still racing from a moment's guilty fright. And suddenly he was embarrassed, ashamed to be found here, by her, in this shabbiness. She shrugged her silver shoulders.

"Why, could we stay apart from carnival, love? All the drunken farmers? Don't you hear them in the streets? All New Hope's at the port celebrating, and so are we." Her face went sober. "Al told me the news. You're recovering your sense."

"News travels too fast. Who else knows?"

"I had it from Al. He's aboard."

"I'd better stray out in that direction too," said Hathaway. "Sam you wait a bit and then you take a casual walk and head for the field too. No baggage. We'll get it if we can. If they get onto us—it could be ugly."

"I'd think so," Merritt agreed, and watched sourly as Hathaway left.

Lilith Courtenay shrugged, hands on hips, walked round the table to put her hand on Merritt's arm. She looked up, pressed his elbow. "Sam, I'm glad, I'm glad you've come to your senses, even if it took you seven long years to do it. Didn't we always tell you what you'd find on Hestia? We tried to warn you."

"Don's found the excuse he was looking for, at least."

Her dark eyes went troubled. "But you agree with

him. You understand how it is here. You *are* going to leave."

"I suppose I am."

"You don't understand these people. They wouldn't be grateful if you tried and failed. They'd likely turn on you and kill you. They're like that. And some of us would miss you if you stayed behind. I would. *I* would. We've been together for seven years."

"No ties, Lil, you always said it."

"It'll be fourteen years before I see Hestia again. If you'd stayed out that five-year contract and gone elsewhere, I'd miss you that round and we'd be near fifty before we had a chance of meeting again. You were a transient. I'm crew. We stay to our own. But that could change. If you were family—'

"That's all right for you, Lil, but I'm not sure it's right for me. You were born to the ship, four or five generations of that kind of life. I'm different. I'm Earthborn."

She laughed soundlessly, a crinkling of the eyes. "Well, part of me is *Adam*; but my mother scattered her affections from Sol to Centauri and back again, and I've never been curious enough to backcount and know. So maybe we have Earth in common, who knows? Would you trade your life for Hestia?"

"I can't think of it clearly. I'm being pushed. I can't make you any promises."

"Can't you? But I don't think I ever asked for any." She gestured toward the windows. "It's a celebration tonight, the end of festival. *Adam's* people are out there, performing another of our many services— seeing that gene pools don't go inbred, you know. And nine months from now there'll be new Hestians, cruel as it is. Carnival is every year for a colonist, years between for us; but this time I've no interest in it. I want you back. You know I wanted your children before we had to split up. I really did. I couldn't imagine letting my first be someone else's. You wouldn't have it. Now—it's different, it's going to be different."

"You could always have chosen to stay with me on Hestia. I waited for that."

She gave a palpable shudder, shook her head. "Some things are too much to ask."

"Poor gypsy. You don't know what it is to call any place home."

"*Adam* is home. Come back to it. We don't love groundlings and we don't love passengers. Come back. Stay. It can be different now."

He nodded slowly. "All right. All right, Lil. You've won. I'm coming. Get out of here, get yourself back to the port. I think it's better you go first and get aboard. It'll be dark in a while. I'll take a walk in that direction toward dusk."

"No. Come now."

"We'd attract attention. Better separately."

"I'm afraid, Sam. I'm afraid of these people."

"Then be careful; and I'll be." He touched her face, kissed her with the casual affection of long acquaintance—it *was* different; the touch lingered; and guilt and wanting were mixed in him, a knot in his stomach. He took her by the arm and turned her for the door. "Go on. Go on, get out of here. The longer you stay, the longer it takes us both getting to the ship. I'll be after you when I know you've had time to get there."

*

17

It was raining again, pelting down in torrents as Hestia's sun slipped from gray day to murky evening. Merritt drew back the curtain and checked the street, found it vacant, nothing but trampled clay and rain-pocked puddles. There was no sound but the fall of water.

He put on his jacket and zipped it up to the chin, stuffed the pockets with personal articles he most treasured, checked the luggage for any item he would miss, and closed it, hoping that the crew would manage to get it aboard all the same, and in a different mind, inclined to beg them not to try, not to risk any hurt to local folk or crew in an argument. He had enough weight on him without that.

The downstairs door slammed open. Steps thundered up, in multitude. *Crew* he thought, anxious for having delayed too long; and then the door opened, and he knew otherwise.

Hestians. Half a dozen of them, brown-clad and bearing the armband of the local police.

"Were you going somewhere, Mr Merritt?"

Merritt stood still, remembered his hand in his pocket and took it out very slowly. He had no weapon. They had sidearms, and truncheons.

"Something I can do for you?" he asked them, hoping that they would still have some reluctance to offend life-giving Mother Earth.

"Governor wants you," said the officer in charge. "Now."

Merritt considered the proposition, the lot of them, the scant chance of dashing through armed police and through a hostile town. There would be crew still outside, the chance of a riot. He reckoned Lilith

Courtenay at the ship, waiting; and that waiting
would grow impatient, would produce inquiries and
action. He trusted so, desperately.

He shrugged, showed empty hands, and went with
them.

Governor Lee was a stout, balding man of gentle
manner; a man perpetually worried, seeming dis-
tracted . . . no figure to inspire fear. Merritt had met
with him, reckoned him and catalogued him; and
those calculations were in shambles. Lee stared him
up and down with that same worried air while the
police lined the room and guarded the door and
Merritt felt very much alone in that moment.

Lee had no reputation, no authority. The briefing
Adam had given indicated twenty years of idleness,
twenty years of starship contacts, meetings with
disdain on the part of crew and abject anxiety on the
part of Lee. There were, in fact, few people accessible
for Lee to govern, and he relied desperately on the
starship supplies and Earth's charity. But of a sudden
the man moved, when all had assured him otherwise,
and that fact alone removed any certainty from the
situation. Merritt folded his hands in front of him
and made no protests; none seemed profitable.

"Sit down, sit down," Lee said.

Merritt did so, stared at Lee across the width of the
desk, met those wrinkle-shrouded eyes and tried not
to break that contact.

"You were running, Mr Merritt."

Merritt said nothing.

"Well," said Lee, "I saw it in your faces the day you

19

landed; and this afternoon—I knew I hadn't won them, but I'd hoped I'd won you, Mr Merritt."

"I was going out to see the town. That's all. Your police—"

"Please, Mr Merritt. You were leaving. We know where the others are. A man is dead, finding that out. It's much easier if we're honest with each other."

"We thought—" The words came out with difficulty. "We thought if we drew back we could talk with you, that you'd believe us then and move out. Governor, you admitted yourself that there's no equipment. Nothing. What do you expect of us?"

"Advice, Mr Merritt. Professional skill. You tell us how and we do the work."

"A colony of five thousand, with no machinery and no manpower to spare. And if you make a mistake, Governor, you'll not get anything. Take my professional advice. Get out of the valley. Better yet, get off Hestia while you can."

"We've asked for weapons, for metal for machinery, and fuel to run it; we've asked for sensors like the equipment you have so we can protect ourselves in the highlands. But we don't get these things. We can't handle them; that's the word we get. It would take the diversion of a starship for several years to support that kind of expedition and five thousand human lives aren't worth that kind of money, are they? We've never had a chance, and they won't jeopardize the finances of the bureau to save Hestia. No, it all comes down to budget. It always does. You prolong your agony, Mr Merritt. That's all your help does."

"Sir—"

The governor's tired eyes focused on his, held. "You

three cared enough to come. What happened? Wasn't the money enough to buy you out?"

"Why won't you give up this colony? Why won't you listen?"

"Can't another groundling understand, Mr Merritt? This is home. It's that simple. And someday the rains will stop again. But it's precious little we have to hold to, with our fields underwater during both growing seasons and no water in winters and fevers in summer."

"You don't have to leave Hestia. The highlands hold what you need. If you'd listened to survey—"

"The highlands also have other inhabitants, Mr Merritt."

Merritt folded his arms and stared at the floor and elsewhere.

"You don't believe."

Merritt shrugged, met Lee's eyes coldly. "Men have always seen ghosts. Maybe they follow us. No, sir. I've heard about them. But survey turned up nothing."

"They're real, Mr Merritt. And there are more of them than of us. They leave their tracks around our farms, they kill our livestock, sometimes break fences or set fires. Sometimes they kill, when we're careless. They're real; and you won't give us weapons and you won't give us sensors. So we stay in the valley. They've given that over to us, and we'll go on holding it while the human race lasts on Hestia. You three were our last real hope; and since you've decided as you have—what do we have left?"

"I'm sorry, sir. But I don't see there's a choice."

"I don't see I have one either. No. No, Mr Merritt.

For once the opportunity belongs to us. I have you here in the town, and I don't think *Adam Jones* is going to do anything about it. If they won't throw a starship off schedule to save five thousand lives, I don't think they'll do it for one man, do you? You're a victim of the same kind of logic as we are, Mr Merritt. I'm very sorry. I certainly don't *want* to do you any harm, but consider my motives. Five thousand lives against the comfort of one: again the logic of numbers."

"*Adam Jones* will leave a marker, and then where will you be? No starship will touch here."

"But we'll have our engineer."

"I can't work alone, sir."

"I wish they hadn't deserted you; I wish they'd been willing to stay; I wish this weren't necessary at all. But that marker beacon might be left whether or not we let you go, mightn't it? And we'd have nothing. We'd die here. We're sorry, Mr Merritt. The move is made. There's no going back from it."

Merritt let go a long breath, leaned back in the chair, considering Lee, the men about him. "I don't like being pushed. Whatever your feelings, I don't like being pushed. I recognize my choices are limited . . . but I still have them."

"Yes."

"I'll make a deal with you then, and keep it."

"What sort of deal, Mr Merritt?"

"You need my cooperation and I want off Hestia. So I'll work at this project for a year, and work at it with the best of my ability, so long as you provide me help. But when that next ship comes, I'll leave on it unless I've been able to find some solution to your problem."

"Your contract specified five years."

"One."

"After the ship leaves, there's really very little reason to have a bargain, is there? If we don't allow it, there's no way you can get near that next ship. You'll live here, with us, as we live. If we don't get that dam built, Mr Merritt, you stay. That's the last and only threat I'll make to you."

"What am I supposed to use for equipment? What I have is on the shuttle."

"Then send for it."

"It won't be enough, even that. You understand that."

Lee made a small and inconsequential gesture. "That's between you and your friends. Ask them. We'll arrange the contact."

"We have alternatives." Don Hathaway's voice said. "Put us through to the governor. We'll make them clear."

"I think they already are," Merritt answered. Static spat. The mansion's communications center, solar-powered, was a patchwork collection of outmoded equipment that must be dusted off once yearly to use with the starships and the shuttles. "Listen to me. We're going to have people dead if you make a move in this direction, and I don't want that. Besides, it's trouble for *Adam*. The Colonial Bureau wouldn't understand a firefight between a starship and her colony. These people are desperate and they'll fight. So just set the gear and the supplies outside the ship. No argument. Please."

"Don't be a martyr, Sam. Give me a sign if you're not talking with a gun to your head."

The guard officer moved, interposed his hand; Merritt held his free of the equipment, made a slight gesture and received permission.

"It's free will, Don. Believe it, sure as we met on station shuttle."

"That's a true sign. All right."

"Wish you were here with me. I could use the help. But that's asking too much, isn't it?"

A silence. "Yes." Hathaway said finally.

"Thought so," Merritt said. His voice felt hollow; the heart of him did. He held a curious lack of bitterness. "Is Lil there?"

"I'm here, Sam."

"Same invitation, Lil. I could use the company."

There was a long pause. "I *can't*," she said finally, miserably.

"I figured that too. No hard feelings."

"I'm sorry, Sam."

It was incredible; it sounded as if she were crying, and that was not at all her habit.

"Goodbye," she said.

The contact went dead.

2

It was misting rain again, the sky over New Hope its usual unappealing gray, the waters colorless from the floating dock to the lagoon to the sky. Merritt descended the wooden steps to the floating dock and paused to turn his hood up against the chill wind that blew here in the open, drenching him.

He had wondered, when they had promised him a boat upriver, just what transportation Hestia could offer. There rode the answer: *Celestine*, broad-bottomed and rearing a tall smokestack amidship. A wheelhouse took up much of the available deck, and the rest of the space was stacked with cordwood and crates of what Merritt took to be his own gear. Often patched and now much in want of another painting, *Celestine* seemed easily half a century old, half as old at least as Hestia.

Merritt looked back, where the governor's police lined the shore, with townsfolk to back them. It was superfluous. The shuttle was gone from the field; *Adam* was gone, the long silence fallen again about Hestia. He shrugged, turned, feeling their collective eyes on his back, and walked the heaving surface to the gangplank, a treacherous bit of board suspended between the moving dock and pitching boat. He made it with a slight stagger, caught his balance again on deck.

A gray-haired man leaned against the wheelhouse, watching him—made no move of welcome, hands in the pockets of his patched coat, unshaven jaw slowly working over a toothpick.

"Amos Selby?" Merritt asked, when the man seemed disposed to stare at him indefinitely.

The Hestian bestirred himself, drew a hand from his pocket and offered it with no show of welcome. "You'll be Mr Merritt, to be sure. Your gear's all aboard."

"Where shall I stay?"

Selby gave a quirk of the mouth that might have been humor. "Well, you'll stay where you can find sitting room, Mr Merritt. Go where you like. We got one deck, got no police here, just water, all around."

There was disturbance on the dock. Footsteps echoed across the wooden planks at high speed: a youth raced down the steps and across the floating landing. Amos grunted.

"My boy," he explained. "Come on, son, hurry it up."

The youth leaped the gap and swept the cap off his blond hair, put it on again straight, and stood staring at Merritt. He was about twenty, almost delicate, and fairer than his father ever could have been. Merritt thought of the starships and the yearly carnival at New Hope, and wondered.

"Sam Merritt—*Mr* Merritt—my boy Jim. Get to work, Jim. We got to get moving sometime today, you know."

"Yes, sir," said Jim, looking contrite, and moved off to take charge of the engine. Amos shook his head and wandered off to the wheelhouse that was four steps up a wooden ladder.

The engine was slowly coaxed to life, a hissing, sluggish museum piece. Merritt walked back to see it work, and Jim looked up at him with a shy grin, but the noise was too much for talking. Jim shouted orders ashore; a pair of men cast them free and the engine began to labor, with Jim running here and there to pull in the cable. *Celestine* slewed out into the current and Merritt walked back to watch the spreading wake, white curl on brown, rain-pocked water, and to stare at the shore. The men became only silhouettes beside a sprawl of brown buildings. The shore dwindled, and the water spread equally on both sides with sand and grass along the banks.

He walked forward then, to the bow, stared out ahead at the countryside and the river, the land flat and flooded and obscured by misting water. The wind cut through the jacket. He shivered finally and threaded his way back to the wheelhouse, climbed the steps to that scant shelter, where Amos plied the wheel. The structure was open, affording view, letting the wind whip down and up and out again.

"It's freezing," Merritt said, teeth clenched.

"Does get a little cold," Amos agreed.

"Do you travel this course in winter too?"

"No way anything moves on Hestia otherwise. Boat's got to come and go."

"How many other boats are there?"

"Five."

"I'm told you know the river best."

"Have to." Amos took the toothpick out of his mouth and pocketed it, as if he had finally made up his mind to converse. "I'm supposed to take you as far as Burns' Station and stay with you. I hear you're supposed to save Hestia."

Merritt sank down on the worn counter that rimmed the side of the wheelhouse, where there was some scant shelter to be had. "I get the impression, Mr Selby, that you don't think much of the business."

"You're the first Earthman in a hundred years to set foot on Hestia and I hear you don't like it much. Myself, I don't trust offworlders much. I don't figure we ever got much from outside."

"I don't figure we ever got much from Hestia, for all that was put into it."

Amos Selby nodded slightly. "True, no denying it, Mr Merritt. But you never needed nothing we could give. So here you are. I suppose we're supposed to owe you something on that account, aren't we?"

Merritt refused to rise to the argument. There seemed no profit in it.

"Well," Amos said finally, "my advice is free for the asking if you have sense enough to want it." He reached for the whistle and blew it sharply, indicated off to port as Merritt stood up to see. A house stood on a hill, tree-rimmed, out of the reach of the river. "James' place there," Amos said. "Used to be a dock there. Nicest place on the river, closest to the city. Dock washed away this fall. They haven't got it rebuilt."

"Do you make regular stops on this run?"

"Not this trip. You're my only cargo. But usually, yes. Some regular, some when I'm flagged in. Everywhere a group of farms can give me a dock. If it wasn't for us rivermen, there'd be no Hestia at all. Many's the time I've had to bring *Celestine* in close to get a family off the porch or had the deck full of sheep and pigs when someone's field's been washed over. We're a stubborn breed, but there's none of us yet learned to breathe water."

Jim brought up tea and sandwiches about noon, into the wheelhouse, the walls of which were cluttered with Merritt's tablets and the corner with a plastic book of charts. Amos slipped a loop on the wheel and kept an eye forward while he ate, pausing to correct course now and again, and now and again to stare at Merritt.

"How old are those?" he asked Merritt finally.

"They're the original survey charts. They're what they gave me to work with."

"You mean the survey a hundred years back?"

"From what you've said and from what I see, I can tell something of the extent of the changes. It's bad. It's a lot worse even than was reported."

Amos washed down a bite of sandwich. "You'll find out more than that. I don't read much: you'll guess that. But I know this valley and this river, and I can show you plenty, how it was and how it is. I can tell you most every sandbar and shift of current from here to Burns' Station."

"And beyond that?"

"No, sir. No one goes up there, and no one will take you there."

"Not for any amount of asking, then?"

"No. No, sir. First of all you'd need to pass white

29

water against the current and there's no boat could
do it. And then you're into uncharted river and wild
country if you made it. No, I'll do whatever errand-
running you want done from the Station to New Hope
and points between, but I value my boat and my own
neck too much to run beyond the Station. I don't
know that I'll convince you of it too early, but there's
times you'll be safest just to take advice untried."

"Is the river open year-round between the Station
and New Hope?"

"Mostly." Amos waved his cup toward the view.
"She'll drop considerable after the fall rains quit.
Then there's sandbars where we're riding now high
and easy. Come spring when the ice melts in the high
country, there'll be pigs swept clear to sea. Then
summers, there's seldom any rain and it's sticky hot.
The killer floods, those are the ones in spring, the
sudden risings. If a man tries to gamble and stay on
his land when it's a question of a few feet of crest
between him and drowning, well, we lose some few
each year that try to outguess the river."

Merritt looked out, braving the wind. The river
was very broad at that point, isolating dead trees and
small hummocks of earth, fence posts and bits of field,
and houses which had ceased to be habitable. Newer
homes could be seen occasionally against the back-
drop of rougher highlands on either side of the river,
fields terraced on the hills. In the north a ragged line
of mountains showed as a gray horizon, bristling with
trees.

"Is that the Upriver you're so afraid of?" Merritt
asked.

"Yonder? Part of it. That's Williams' Heights there,

just big forest. Myself, I don't trust any forest, but there's some with the nerve to bed down next to it. Trouble is, it runs on and on forever, right into the Upriver itself, and what lives in the Upriver can live there too, for all you know. I don't like places like that at all; no one does; but there's not so much land left now that folks can be choosy. Some even get brave enough to cut a few trees into the deep forest and clear them new land."

"What's to stop them?"

Amos gave him one of those guarded looks and bit thoughtfully at the sandwich, swallowed again. "Well, Mr Merritt, it's just well known on Hestia there's things in the forest that don't like axes; and some of them are downright clever about showing it. Little trees nobody misses; but you cut down a big one, now, a really old one, well, your fences could fall down or your livestock could die or your house could catch fire."

"Truth?"

"Truth. And another truth, friend—when you start building your dam up at Burns' Station and backing a lake up into the Upriver, you're going to flush a few things out of there that none of us are going to want for neighbors. But the lake has to be. We'll solve the other problem when it meets us on our own grounds."

"Maybe the dam shouldn't be built there. Maybe it would be better to create several smaller reservoirs upriver."

"Huh. You'll get Hestians into the Upriver when rain falls up."

"Because you're convinced something lives up there. But you tell me then, Mr Selby, how a group of minded beings could have been missed in the first survey and then live next to a human colony for a hundred years without leaving something in the way of tangible evidence they exist."

"We got plenty of evidence. Dead men and livestock."

"Animals could do that. It doesn't take sapients."

"Didn't claim they was human. But clever and mean, yes. Friend, you're in the middle of civilization right now. When you've lived next to an Upriver woods for a month or so, you'll believe in a lot of things." He galvanized himself into sudden action, put down the food and took the wheel, for they were coming into shallow water, little ripples to the starboard side. A house sat on that side, between trees and inlets of floodwater. Heaps of flood-borne brush were banked along the highwater mark, and what land was not flooded was pitted with small lakes permanent enough to grow reeds in profusion.

"See that place?" Amos asked.

"Looks like that farm is lost."

"You set foot out there and you'd go in up to your knees even where it looks solid. Can't work it any more, no way. Only survival crops will grow there now, and that just summertime vegetables. Nothing much. The river used to keep its banks here and this was a beautiful farm. There were levees and a house nearer the river when I was a boy. They lost two children when the first house went. Rebuilt then. The old man lost his wife in the flood this spring. Now he sits in that house with the windows all out and not enough to eat, and takes shots at anyone that comes onto his land. He may be dead now. I passed this way

by night and didn't see a light. So he's likely gone, or
out of lights. Same with this whole forsaken riverside. We know the score, but it's our world, and we'll
stay in spite of all them that try to make us go. You
want to understand Hestia, friend outsider, well,
understand that old man. Understand us that lets
him stay. We got no use for Earthmen and Earthmen's attitudes. Mother Earth ain't our mother, and
I don't know why you come out here, but I'm sure
you've found out by now that we haven't got it. We're
a little touchy in temper; a lot shy of outsiders' help.
But you help us on our terms: *that's* help. That's help
we can do with. Maybe you got the sense to see that.
I hope so."

"If I have to build where you say build, I can't
guarantee anything; but if that's the way you want
it, that's what you'll get. I'll tell you my opinion on
it, but I'll do it if that's my only choice."

"You know, there ain't a man or woman on Hestia
that don't know they could pack up and ride the next
starship out. But no one's done it, not one. We're
stubborn. We stay."

"You think you have the resources to stop the
river?"

Amos frowned. "Well, about that, I don't know. I
seen the river win every round so far. But we just
give a little when it does."

Merritt had expected the boat to tie up at some dock
to spend the night: it was a good many days' traveling
to Burns' Station. But well after dusk she was still
running along at a much reduced speed, with nothing
in sight but the distant lonely lights of an occasional

house on the southside ridge. The slap and suck of water at the moving hull, the monotonous slow sound of the engine, were all alone in the dark. *Celestine* held the center of the channel, with one dim lamp burning outside the wheelhouse.

At last, while Amos took the wheel again after a long rest, Jim opened up the only cabin space *Celestine* had, a low-ceilinged and poorly ventilated hold under the wheelhouse, into which it was only possible to crawl. Jim went first; Merritt followed, found thin mattresses and a nest of sheets, cushioning from the bare planking. A little light found its way through louvers, and a cold wind relieved the stifling warmth; but the engine made a deafening racket and sent a vibration through the very planking of the deck, making sleep doubtful.

"It's the best we got, Mr Merritt," said Jim. "I know you're used to better, but that deck gets cold before morning. There's more comfort here."

Merritt worked his way to the center of one pallet, and fought the sheet and blanket into order in the dark. The sweat began to run on his face. He rolled onto one arm in the narrow space and began to work himself out of the jacket and boots, with the slow chug of the engine jarring his bones. "Do you go at this by shifts, you and your father?"

"Yes, sir. At least on this stretch, where there's no safe dock to tie up to. Can't run a cable to shore just anywhere, 'less you're willing to take on all sorts of pests. That's why Dad and me do most of our sleeping by daylight. Safer that way."

Merritt turned on the pallet, drawing a single sheet up against the roughness of the blanket. "I guess there might be something in it. I don't seem to appreciate just what you do have to contend with—or a lot else on Hestia, for that matter."

"It must be something—to travel aboard one of the starships."

Merritt frowned at the unexpectedly wistful tone, regarded the boy curiously in the barred light from the louvers. "I didn't think Hestians entertained such ideas," he said, and almost before the last word had left his mouth he guessed he should not have said it.

"Did they tell you that?" the youth asked, suspicion hard in his voice.

"What?"

"That I'm half offworlder? Or does it stand out that bad?"

"No, no one mentioned it. I didn't know it."

The boy sank back, bars of light rippling over face and arm and into dark. "No matter, then. Forget it."

"Do you ever think of taking one of those shuttles off Hestia?" Merritt asked.

"No." And a moment later: "That's a lie. But I got too much here and too little elsewhere. There's a lot of down-river Hestians that have my kind of beginning; and they just stay downriver Hestians—which ain't much, if you know Hestia. New Hope's a sinkhole. But this old river—he's something else. *This* is Hestia. You don't know us till you know the upper valley. And that's the thing the starships have never touched.—Yes, I've thought of leaving. I've thought of it every year I watch one of those big silver ships go up out of sight. But I got no idea what they go to, and I know that the Millers and the Burnses and so on are waiting for *Celestine*. So we're back upriver again."

3

Burns' Station hove up against a cloud-rimmed sky, sun-stained wisps of fleece against black, bristling hills, and the station itself less farm than hill-fort, house and girdling walls and outstructures of stone set high on a promontory where the river bent. The facing height was dark with woods, but the trees were cleared back at a considerable distance on the occupied side, providing a measure of farmland and pasturage.

Dusk was settling thick by the time *Celestine* chugged in to the floating dock. Two blasts of the whistle brought a stir of life from the hill, gates opening, lantern-bearing men hastening down the face of the promontory on wooden steps.

There was no lack of hands to receive the cables: Jim hurled one coil from the bow and Merritt cast the second from the stern, hastened to help Jim run out the plank, while the engine fell away into silence and Amos joined them at the gangway.

Hands reached to steady them, friendly faces lantern-lit, all male and most bearded. Jim went first and shook hands and pounded shoulders; Merritt followed into the commotion, ignored for Amos, who came after. "Engineer," Amos said of him, and there was a cheer and no scarcity of hands held out in welcome.

"My equipment," Merritt protested as the lantern-bearers began to climb; but some men stayed and began to unload for them, and he let himself be guided up the wandering board steps, up and up to the station's open gates.

Another group waited inside them, in the dirt yard, where there was a blaze of torches, where slits of windows in the stone house showed yellow of firelight, and big square windows on the upper floors blazed friendlier welcome.

A great red-haired fellow came out from the rest to Amos and grasped his offered hand in friendly violence, then looked at Merritt, face frozen in a remnant of a smile.

"Frank," said Amos, "meet Sam Merritt. We got ourselves an Earthman engineer. —Sam, this here's Frank Burns. *The* Burns, head of station."

Burns grinned pleasantly and thrust his big hand toward Merritt. "So they heard us. But—" he asked suddenly, looking beyond them to the others, "wasn't there supposed to be more of you? You got no crew, no helpers?"

"I'm afraid not," said Merritt.

"Wait a minute now," said a balding man to Burns' left. "Earth promised us at least two men and a work crew."

"I'm sorry," said Merritt. "I'm all you've got."

There was an angry murmuring from some present, that made Merritt suddenly doubt his welcome and his safety, but Burns set a heavy hand on his shoulder and looked at the man who had objected.

"Mr Merritt," Burns said, "want you to meet Tom Porter. Tom's a neighbor of ours, come up to wait out what *Celestine*'d bring us. Tom Porter's holding's big as ours and right next, lots of families in Porter's Station, but they use our landing."

"Mr Porter." Merritt accepted the offered hand.

"Glad to meet you," Porter said, belated grace. "Fact is, we're glad to get any help at all, but we'd hoped for more."

"I wish I had help too," Merritt said. "But I'm told you can supply manpower and some supplies; we've precious little of the latter."

"We'll manage," said Burns. "Hey, I don't know what we're standing out here in the wind for. Ken, Fred, you boys set what gear there is in the shed, and baggage in the main room, anywhere you like. —You timed it right, Amos; Hannah's just got dinner on the table."

"Good," Amos grinned. "Been looking forward to a winter with Hannah's cooking. How's things here?"

"All right. Mostly all right." Frank Burns hailed them into the open doorway of the big main house, into light and warmth; and behind them the outer gates creaked shut and most of the crowd followed.

It was a grander house, in its stone and bare-beams style, than the governor's mansion in New Hope; and it was newer. The floors were split planking, massively solid; the walls were hung with necessities, rope and other such items; the furniture was hand-hewn and use-smoothed, and the air smelled of woodsmoke and savory food. Oil lamps and an enormous fireplace gave light, cast shadows back into retreating hallways and to a balconied upstairs. Women and children hastened this way and that setting the table; an ignored baby screamed indignation. Outside, cattle lowed and sheep bleated; and inside, human voices shouted over the confusion.

"We're hotel as well as farm," said Burns. "The last place on the river, the highest ground in flood: half a dozen farms round about do their meetings here and their trading at our dock, and come here when it floods. Same with Tom's place downriver. How long do you figure to stay over, Amos? Did I hear you say all winter?"

"Don't really know," Amos answered. "I'm supposed to stay by our friend here and provide him the use of a boat when needed . . ." He paused to grin at some elderly acquaintance and to shake hands and exchange words briefly. They were the center of all the gathering now, old and young clustered about them, the children dancing about and asking for some treat brought from downriver. It was impossible to talk at length. "Give it up," Burns said when Amos tried further. "Shed the coats and sit."

Merritt unzipped the jacket and surrendered it to a child who held out her hands for it, turned tableward and let himself be placed near the head of the long board, next Burns himself and Amos and Porter, and Jim on the other side. An older woman came up drying her hands on an apron and offered her own welcome. "Hannah Burns," she said of herself, the while a boy shouldered in at Merritt's other side to put down a cup of tea, and food was appearing in huge bowls and kettles, seized and passed one to the next with great care.

"A pleasure, Hannah Burns," Merritt said. "Sam Merritt. Thank you for making room for us."

Hannah Burns gave a short nod and something caught her quick eye: she shouted a name and instructions about serving and was off again. Merritt blinked, noting the unbroken line of male faces at table: neither women nor children. All at once there was the feeling of difference, his own manners, his machine-woven clothes and smooth-shaven face an alien distinction.

"How soon," asked Porter, leaning forward with a spoon in hand, "how soon you going to get started, Mr Engineer?"

Merritt paused to let the girl making the rounds with the kettle of stew ladle some past his shoulder to his plate, thanked her with a nod and leaned forward again. "Well, as soon as I can. It'll take me some little time to look over the possible sites—"

"*We* did the looking," Porter shot back. "We don't have the time for you to take five years at this project, Mr Merritt. We got families down there in the lower valley that are going to be washed out next spring, that are praying now the floods don't get worse before winter stops them. We need help now, quick. We got no time to wait."

Of a sudden the table chatter had fallen away. The bustle of women and children faded. The whole room was listening. Only the barking of a dog sounded outside.

"If what we build doesn't hold," said Merritt, "I

don't need to tell you what will happen next spring. *That* would be a disaster, Mr Porter."

"I think," said Burns from the head of the table, "the site we have in mind is a good one. It's just half a mile upriver from here, where the canyon narrows the river down. There's a good deal of rock there to be used, and the canyon splits the upper valley basin from the lower. We can't get men or supplies any farther into the Upriver, and building the dam down-river would wipe out the best farmland we've got."

"It sounds reasonable," said Merritt. "But I'll still have to see the place myself before I can start making any plans. I'm aiming at a spring deadline too, Mr Porter. I saw enough of what you're talking about on the way up the river that I very much understand what you mean. But I don't want to waste our limited supplies or risk lives and property by jumping into this without study. I can promise you I'm going to be working steadily from now on, and by the time the water falls so that we can start working, I hope to have some plans drawn up. You can help now by finding a crew to work."

"Burns and I can raise a thousand in a month," said Porter. "Do you need more than that?"

It was a fifth the total population of Hestia. Merritt considered the two of them, one side and the other. "What we'll need depends on the time and the site and the amount of rock we'll have to move."

"You'll have all the help we can give," Burns assured him. "You understand, Mr Merritt—we've seen a lot of land and no few of our friends and relatives lost to that river. It doesn't get easier to be patient, knowing we're within sight of an answer. I can't tell you how anxious we all are to see this project underway, but we understand the difficulty involved. We've tried it twice ourselves and lost."

"Well, I'll get out to that site of yours first thing tomorrow and see what I can learn."

Burns made a deprecating gesture. "No, no, Mr Merritt. Take a day to catch your breath; I'm hurrying no guest out into the edge of Upriver. I've got some charts of our own may interest you, and lists of the supplies we've been storing toward this project for years."

"Frank," said Hannah Burns, coming to lean on the man's chair-back, "I'm sure those things can wait til late tomorrow. Let 'em eat in peace, for pity's sake. I'm sure they're tired." She lifted her eyes to Merritt, smiled tautly with a crinkling of sun-wrinkles. "Room's waiting on you. Good meal and steady land underfoot and you'll be wanting it. Trust it more than old river: good walls and lots of folk around you. You'll sleep here, no worry."

After cramped, sweltering nights and cold days on *Celestine*, the little room upstairs in Burns' house was luxury: quaint, with the same rough furniture and handmade rugs and a pillow-soft bed. Merritt tested it fully clothed, lay back in it with the billowing mattress rising about him and shut his eyes a moment, opened them again to watch yellow lamp-light flickering on dusty beams. *Adam Jones* seemed incredible from such a perspective.

A wood stove gave heat, too much heat, and the room was close. Merritt rolled out of the yielding mattress and went to the shuttered window, unbarred and opened it, inhaling the clean, free wind out of the dark . . . leaned there, looking out. There was a view of a slanting, shingled roof, and after a little gap, the roof of a shed, and an irregular portion of the yard, then the stone wall and the forest. A torch gleamed, moved, vanished. The yard, the whole house was settling for the night. The noise downstairs had sunk away.

He turned away, opened the luggage that one of Burns' folk had set beside the door and began to unpack, considered the task of arranging his belongings for a moment and gave it up, hung out only what he meant to wear on the morrow, and set his shaving kit on the table.

Someone came up the hall—traffic came and went with the house arranging itself for the night; but the steps stopped and someone knocked.

"Come in," he said, half-turned, and found a young woman there, her arms full of towels. Her first glance was to him, the second to the open window, and she deposited the towels on the bed and went at once to the window, closed it and the shutters, fastening them with the bar.

"I'm sorry," she said. "That's awfully dangerous, to sleep that way. We keep the windows shuttered at night and the doors bolted."

"Thank you," he said, taken aback.

"Meg Burns," she said, smiling suddenly. "Daughter."

He had seen her downstairs, but the lights had been poor. Standing next the lamp as she was, her red-brown hair acquired a brightness, her brown eyes a gentleness that stopped one for an extra glance. No competition for *Adam Jones'* light-of-love daughters, perhaps, but there was a healthiness about her that had its proper place in wind and sun, not a starship's sterile atmosphere.

"I brought the towels," she said. "There's a bath down the hall at the end and hot water on the stove there; you refill it for the next and don't dump the tub till has to be. And I'm sorry about the window, but the light draws all kinds of pests. —If you wake up for breakfast in the morning it's ready at daybreak. Just come downstairs. There's always enough. Or sleep over. That's no matter either."

"Thank you," he murmured a second time, and Meg Burns turned to go, smiled at him over her shoulder as he smiled at her, then was off down the hall outside with a patter of slippered feet.

He closed the door after, considered the closed window and put the towels on the table, looked again to the door.

Not the manners he had known, he decided, reckoning the way of things at table, the implications in the house of order of a different sort than he easily guessed: caution settled on him, a conviction that there were borders and barriers here.

He tried the bath, in line after one of the Burnses: the way was to learn who was next and knock on that door when finished. The bare-boards room was stiflingly hot and humid, and there was no plumbing but a drain in the floor and an admonition posted to empty only washwater down.

And in the morning, with a pain in his muscles from the too-soft mattress, he considered his outworlder clothes and his outworlder manners and still shaved, still dressed as he would have aboard the *Adam Jones*. He had his own ways, and purposed to keep them.

Daylight put a bright complexion on the fortress-station and on all the land about it. His belly full of a fine breakfast (he had been late, but Hannah Burns had saved eggs and sausage for him, a special case among her guests), Merritt climbed the grassy slope to the crest of the promontory over the river, his hands jammed in the pockets of his jacket, for there was a chill in the morning wind, more than he had known on the river.

The clouds were entirely gone, leaving a sky of brilliant blue, a pale morning sun too small for the sky, a landscape of unsuspected colors sprawling out in the first clear daylight he had seen on Hestia: oranges and yellows and bluegreens of autumn in this alien woods, with no rain to curtain them.

At the base of the promontory the river ran rough from the narrows, yellow-brown with silt. *Celestine* bobbed at her moorings at the dock that was sheltered by the bending of the river, toy boat on a river gone miniature. A sound of water came up the deep, a trick of the air currents.

Against the northern and eastern sky rose more mountains than he had yet seen, a bristling outline usually hidden by the rains: foothills of the Divide, source of floods and barrier that made the weather. It was the Upriver, at least part of it, its nearer approaches mantled in dark forest.

The wind grew bitter. Merritt turned his shoulder to it and pulled his hood up, glanced back at the station's rambling walls, at the fields and the meadow downslope. Two of the women sat with the sheep, while a black dog and a brown one trotted the limits of the flock.

It was a way to walk, a lee side out of the wind: Merritt made a slow and casual descent, and when he had come nearer the herders and the sheep, he recognized one of the two shepherdesses in coveralls for Meg Burns.

She saw him at a distance and waved a hand in tentative greeting. He ventured out across the dew-wet grass, walking carefully among the skittish sheep, causing work for the dogs, who worked them back together.

"Good morning," he said to the women, and both, seated on a bare space of rock, gave him polite nods of welcome. Meg stood up then, regarded him in her own way as warily as did the brown dog who came to sit at her side.

"Making up your mind where you're going to build?" she asked him.

"I've been looking at the charts and thinking on it." He gave a perfunctory smile at the half-grown girl who was Meg's companion, looked back to Meg. "Do you know the river beyond this point?"

"Not well," she said. "I don't go there. No one does."

"Have you lived here all your life?"

"I was born here," she said, and smiled in a way that made her ordinary face beautiful. "I'm afraid we're not travelers. I've never been anywhere at all."

"What, not even to New Hope?"

"No," she said, "not even to the next farm."

"Don't you sometimes worry about living right here on the edge of the human world?"

She laughed silently, as though the question surprised her. "Not really. Not often. Our place has always been safe, our walls keep us that way, and most of the things in the forest are afraid of the dogs. We're all right if we come away from the forest before dark and never take the big trees. We're agreeable to it and it doesn't bother us; that's how we live here. We fit in."

"Things might change when the river changes, you know."

"I know. But that has to be, after all. Everything will change. But then maybe Hestia will be somewhere worthwhile. Maybe Earth will send us more help then." She looked out over her flock, whistled and pointed, and the dogs ran, headed off a stray from the edge. She turned then, looked back at him. "I've grown up here," she said. "And for most of my life we've been waiting for you. I'd almost given up."

To that, he did not precisely know what to say. It was, in all, a better argument than the governor had used.

"Do you think," he asked, "that you could show me the place your father thinks we ought to build? Is it too far?"

She looked a little doubtful, looked into his face as if she were estimating him. "All right," she agreed after a moment. "But you'd better go back to the house after a gun."

4

"This is it," said Meg Burns, balancing surefootedly on a pinnacle of rock. The dog scurried about the brush in the forest behind them and started nothing but birds.

Merritt looked down where the water boiled white far beneath them, and up to the valley which had been invisible from the point at Burns' Station.

The crest on which the station stood and this narrows where they now were formed a natural barrier between two great valleys. A dam was indeed possible here, at least by first sight. The eastern valley would be destroyed, almost totally inundated up to the steep slopes of its wooded mountains, but men on Hestia had a great deal of land from which to choose. Now it was a glory of autumn colors, of rock spires and tall conifers.

"It's a shame to do it," he said, looking about him, "but I suppose there's not much other choice, even granted we could get a boat up past that narrows, . . ."

"There's rocks," said Meg. "We had an accident back a few years ago when we were trying to build on our own: one of the boats hit a rock and blew up. The boiler exploded and everyone aboard was killed.

Twenty people. I don't think you could ever talk Amos into going up to the edge of that. Besides, the high valley is full of troubles. It's not a pleasant kind of place at all, and you wouldn't get men to carry supplies across it."

"It's some country, all right." Merritt cast a look eastward, where the tops of trees lay like a mottled carpet as far as the mountain-skirts, a bluegreen and orange expanse cut by the veinwork of streams and the river itself. There came no sound but the distant rush of water and the wind sighing through the leaves ... the occasional rustle of the brown dog which accompanied them and coursed off on her own business in the thickets.

"Lonely," said Meg after a moment. "Is it like Earth? Is it anything the same?"

It struck him with an eerie feeling, that this Hestian would have to ask: a century removed from the mother-world, they had all a slightly separate accent and named with earthly names things which were only superficially like their earthly counterparts—having forgotten, perhaps, the original. The colonial program had birthed something it perhaps had not planned: a generation of men who had no understanding of Earth.

"It's like," he said, "or it used to be. There's little wild land left there now."

She looked at him with the hint of a frown. "You must think we're very backward."

"I've no complaints."

"Why would you have come out here?"

"The governor persuaded me."

"But why all this way to Hestia in the first place? It's a long way to come, for the sake of strangers."

"Well, my reasons seven years ago were different from those that got me upriver, and maybe after a little while my reasons will change again."

She gave him a sideward glance, settled on a faint smile. The light red-brown of her hair and the flush of her cheeks and the slight freckling from the sun were the colors of Hestia itself. He had not thought her strikingly beautiful when he first saw her: it was like something he had privately discovered, in the sun and the slight crinkling of a smile. He wondered her age: nineteen, twenty, perhaps; and whether she knew what effect she had on a lonely man.

"We ought to get back," she said, suddenly breaking away from his eyes, and clapped her hands to call the dog. "My dad will worry if we're gone out here too long. They'll be sending searchers out."

"You don't take walks much, I take it."

"No, oh, no," she said, and bent to clear a branch. "We're still within reach of home right now, but just at the foot of the rocks down there, that's where the Upriver starts. That's the end of it. That's the line we never cross."

The sleeping house was quiet, no light showing under the crack of the door. Merritt lay stone-still a moment, at last lifted his head from the pillow, plagued by the indefinable sensation of having heard or felt something. There were noises, but only the expected ones, boards giving with the weather, the sighing of the wind at the window, something that went bump in time with the gusts.

A dog barked, suddenly, hysterically; and sheep and cattle outside surged against their pens, bleating and bawling in wild panic. Steps crossed downstairs at a run and someone took a clapper to a metal pan and started beating on it. It rang like doomsday and Merritt came out of bed wide awake now, scrambling for his clothes and his boots and his gun.

He reached the balcony of the main room armed and half dressed at the same instant as Porter and Meg and some of the other residents. Merritt followed them, scrambling downstairs with others coming behind and more assembling out of the downstairs wings, men and women in night-dress scurrying about checking bolts and bars.

"Hey!" someone yelled at Merritt. "You got your window closed and bolted?"

"Yes," he called back.

"One of you girls double-check those upstairs windows in the hall," Burns shouted. "Hey, Amos— where do you think you're going?"

Amos Selby was struggling into his coat, and Jim likewise, already heading for the door. "I got my ship down there," Amos said, "and I got too much at stake with it to sit up here."

Jim was with his father as he unbarred the main door and ran; and Merritt hesitated in confusion what the threat might be. But he was certain that he had in his own modern gun a far more effective weapon than the two Hestians carried, and that Amos and Jim were doing something rash. He snatched someone's coat from the peg and ran out after them into the dark yard, trying to overtake them both before they could leave the security of the walls. Someone behind them was cursing all of them and ordering him to stop, whether from anger at the coat or from fear; he heard men running after them.

Amos reached the main gate and hauled up the securing bar, let himself and Jim through to the outside, and it was there that Merritt overtook them and the Porters caught up with all of them from behind. There was a view of the river from the gate, with the steps lacing back and forth down the steep face of the hill; and the first thing evident was that *Celestine* was free of her cables and headed downcurrent sideways.

Amos cursed under his breath and started running—old man that he was, he could run; and headed off the slanting side of the promontory across the grassy descent toward the trees and the bending of the river.

Merritt saw what he was trying to do, in overtaking *Celestine*; but the course was going to take them through brushy areas and past a dozen opportunities for ambush, and the current was faster than they could possibly run.

Jim came in at a tangent and skidded downslope, cutting ahead by a little, lost for the moment in brush.

"It's no good," Merritt yelled after them in despair. "Give her up. It's no good killing yourself."

Amos paid him no heed, ran stumbling onward until he could go no farther and pulled up holding his chest; but Jim kept going.

"You got a gun," Amos gasped when Merritt stopped for him. "You stay with my boy. He hasn't."

Merritt hurled himself off then, trying to overtake

Jim; Porter was close with him, though some of the others had stopped for Amos. Jim stayed ahead, a flitting shadow in the brush, refusing their cries to stop.

The river broke sharply to the left just ahead: and *Celestine* had stopped. They came on her aground on a bar, her dark bulk discernible against the moonlit water.

Jim stopped among the saplings on the shore; Merritt overtook him, and so did Porter and his men. "She's not bad," Jim said, and began stripping out of his coat. "I'll get out to her."

"Hold it, boy," Porter said. "No telling what you might meet aboard."

"Somebody's got to get out to her," said Jim. "I'll make it all right and the People never yet went around machinery. I'll start her up and see if I can't work her off that bar."

"You be careful, boy," Porter said.

"Yes, sir." Jim handed Merritt his coat; and Merritt tried to shape some objection, but none would organize itself: he knew the rivermen too well. It was their life and livelihood sitting out there; and it belonged to Amos, and Jim, half a son, could not lose it.

A slender figure in the moonlight, Jim stepped down to water's edge and tried the temperature of it, bent over a few moments to get his wind before attempting it. Then he stepped off into the black waters and went in up to his waist.

Gingerly he waded out, not yet having to swim. Once, twice, the dark spot in the water that was Jim's head went out of sight, then reappeared; he was swimming now, fighting the current.

Amos joined them, helped along through the brush by one of Porter's kin, and shook his way free to come down to the bank to watch.

"Jim'll get her," said Porter softly. "Don't worry, Amos. We got her now."

"You think I worry about her more than for my boy?" Amos returned shortly, and then kept quiet and watched, for Jim had reached the boat and disappeared into the shadow. There was a murmur of anxiety on the bank. Then Jim reappeared, clambering up the cable by the stern; and there was a general exhaling of breath among the group on the shore.

Time passed. There was no sound from the boat. No one spoke or cracked a twig.

"I'll get her started," Jim's voice called back suddenly. "But I'm afraid it may not be enough to get her off. She's riding too steady to be much adrift."

"You be careful out there, boy," Amos shouted. "Are you alone on that boat?"

"Yes, sir, far as I can tell, I am. Don't worry. If need be, I can ride her out till dawn and we can get some men out here. If she breaks free again, so much the better. I think her bottom's sound."

"Did she break or was she cut?" Porter called out.

"She was cut," Jim replied.

The engine started, but it was as Jim feared. She could not quite drag herself free. Cable had to be carried ashore and back again, and it was well after dawn before *Celestine* could finally winch herself off the bar and into clear water.

It was cold, killing work. At last, with *Celestine* freed and chugging her deliberate way back upriver to the dock, the crew on the bank started back for the station uphill, blind with exhaustion and half-frozen. There was talk of nothing but dry clothes and breakfast and sleep, in that order, and Merritt flexed skin-stripped palms and agreed with them; there was no feeling in his feet and more than enough in his back, but it was salve to his aches when one of the Porters clapped him on the shoulder and allowed that he was due a drink when they all caught their breath.

They were staggering when they reached the crest, where Burns and his folk held the open gate.

"We just about lost her," Porter said to Burns, when they reached that security, and looked down the height where the boat was slowing putting in to dock.

Burns gave a long breath, a jerk of his head to the way below. "Earthman—you come down to the dockside. There's something I want to show you."

Merritt opened his mouth to protest, indignant at being turned from the gate. He was too tired even to contemplate climbing steps down and up again; but having the boat back and being one with these folks set him in a biddable mood . . . and it was too late: Burns was on his way without pausing for his opinions.

He followed, on numb feet and shuddering knees. At the bottom of the steps Burns waited for him to catch his breath, and waited for him again a short distance farther, off the boards and where the clay of the bank was soft with moisture.

"There," Burns said, pointing down. "There. Have a look, friend, and learn what we've been talking about when we say we don't go into the Upriver.

Many a one I've seen, but none quite so clear and plain."

Printed deep in the rain-soft clay, as one would lean against that bank to catch balance in descending, was the print of a long-fingered hand, a hand with an opposable thumb, but with bones too elongate to belong to a man or woman or child. A few yards below, at the end of a sliding mark, was a footprint of the same proportions as the hand and toed like a man's.

The prints continued downslope toward the floating dock, where severed ropes were still looped about the moorings, and a handful of Burnses were ready to receive cable from *Celestine*.

5

It was one of those blue-ceilinged days that were growing increasingly frequent with the coming of winter. The trees were either bare now, or held the last few leaves, stark skeletons of white among the blue-green shadow of conifers, and the land had gone all brown and yellow, the woods thickly blanketed with leaves that rustled dustily dry.

Notebook in hand, Merritt took the lower trail down to the river's edge around the bending of the promontory. The river was now far lower than it had been at his arrival. Rocks once submerged now stood well above the waterline, and there was a safe ledge to use in skirting the water. It would be possible to get a line across to the other side, with *Celestine's* help and a little effort on the part of the men; and from that line a footbridge could be begun, to span the gorge. It was going to be necessary to do a great deal of traveling from one side of the site to the other.

He descended to the very edge of the water, walking carefully because of the slickness of the rocks, where white froth curled up to the soles of his boots. And in his mind, gazing at the narrows, he saw the structure that was going to take shape across the throat of that chasm; and the vast lake it was going to make behind it: spillways to let the overflow go, water for fields in season, safety for downriver, the river tamed to the service of man.

Once the river kept its banks, once there was dry and dependable land, Hestia could start to grow. Boats could move at will on the lower course, and even ply the lake in safety; crops would come up in abundance, rail and river transport could move them, making full use of the steam engine that was Hestia's chief source of power now. Electricity would follow, water-given and solar, and humans live in light and warmth. And beyond that, the world would make itself a respectable colony, a mote of an oasis in the course of starships: all if they could make this one beginning.

All if they had time.

A rustling disturbed the leaves farther up the trail. Nails clicked on stone. Merritt whipped his pistol out and turned, heart pounding, until he saw only brown Lady, tail wagging merrily, come panting up to him. He put the gun away and caressed the dog's silky head.

"Well," he said to the dog. "where's your mistress, eh?"

And a moment more brought Meg Burns down the trail, following Lady.

"Hello," said Meg, dropping down to the ledge on which he stood.

"Don't make up to me," he said. "Didn't I tell you I don't like your coming out to this place alone? You used to have good sense."

She grinned and came into his arms, a pleasant

bundle of soft leather and furs and homespun, for the air was cold. He kissed her on the lips and set her back again.

"That dog isn't much protection to you, you know," he told her. "She's not very fierce."

"You don't have anyone at all out here with you. And you stay out so late, all alone."

"I'm armed; you're not."

"That's all right. I don't like guns, and Lady's my ears. —What have you decided out here all by yourself? Why did you send the men back?"

"Because there was nothing more for them to do here today, and I'm trying to make up my mind what to do next."

"What is that, then?"

He sat down on a rounded rock and made room for her close beside him, put his arm about her. "Well," he said, "you know what Porter's sentiments are. He wants that dam built by this spring. And I'm not so sure. I have some thoughts we could do a makeshift job this year, yes, but it's going to rush us. A little more planning, a little more certainty—but you see, if we don't get started right now, there's a good chance we won't beat the spring rains. Porter's been breathing down my neck these last two weeks—had one of his men on the site today that was driving me to the bitter edge. The fellow won't understand what I tell him. He sees it's possible; I see it's dangerous. What do you think, Meg? Do we take the gamble or can we wait?"

"Why ask me? What can I know?"

"Where it concerns Hestia, a lot more than I do. Can the valley survive another year? All I know is what the river's likely to do, nothing more. Is Porter right and am I wrong in wanting to wait, in wanting to catch it at summer low and wait a few months?"

She looked down into the water, unwilling to speak for a moment. "Sam," she said, "it's really chancy, isn't it?"

"It's chancy. And if they want me to gamble everything, lives, property, all the supplies hoarded for this project over years of waiting—it's not like I'm delaying for my own advantage. They've promised me I can be free of my contract whenever I get a dam finished."

There was a sudden tension in her; he felt it. She looked up at him, brown eyes hurt.

"Meg, I don't want to do things that way. I have a few interests here. Personal interests." He drew a smile from her with that, and her arms went about him.

It was quiet there with the river murmuring below them, drowning even forest sounds; and very lonely, only old Lady lying there watching them. He gathered Meg closer and she snuggled against him, warm and soft and content, leaving him to think thoughts that he had put off time and again.

"Neither of us," he said finally, "has any good sense being out here."

"There's no being alone up at the house. Since those men started arriving, there's always someone underfoot."

"Haven't you been told better than to stay too close to offworlders?"

"Yes," she said, a warm breath against his neck, "but you're not leaving, Sam. You'd better not."

"In that case, we'd better both think of the consequences." He thought one way and then the other, and finally sighed and took her arms, put her back from him and looked into her eyes. "You're not one of the starship people; you're Hestian right to your moral little heart, and you know it. And back-country Hestian at that. You don't go down to meet the ships. It's not your way, Meg."

"I don't want to lose you." Her voice came very faint, a scant moving of her lips. "You won't be leaving when you're done, will you? Sam, you never talked about leaving."

"Forget that. No. But forget the rest of it too, until we've settled other things. Until the dam is standing. My future on Hestia isn't all that certain until then. And to be honest, Meg, you just don't know me that well."

"I think I do."

"*What* do you know? That I'm from the other side of the sun and that's attractive to your romantical ideas? That I'm different and that makes me special?"

"And you think I'm a little girl from nowhere, who's going to get herself involved with you to keep you, and you're trying to keep me from making a mistake because I don't know any better. You're a kind man, Sam. Sometimes you're too kind."

Meg could cry charmingly, just a single tear slipping down her cheek. Merritt shook his head in despair, wiped it away and drew her tight against him until she stopped shivering.

"Well," he told her softly, "you're not far wrong, but I don't think you give yourself enough credit, Meg, not near enough. See, you think of me, and I have to

think of you, and I'm not going to talk you into
something you could regret. I'm not so sure you might
not change your mind about a lot of things if I should
have to leave Hestia, or if something goes wrong.
Don't argue with me. Come on, right now. I'm taking
you home."

"I don't care what people think."

"*I* care what they think about you." He set her on
her feet and put his arm about her again, starting
upslope toward the trail. "You don't make my nights
any the more peaceful. I think about—staying. If the
dam works, if—*if* this world will have me, if . . . so
many things. I could be persuaded to stay, if a lot of
things work together. But not at your expense. Not—
tied here in an uncertain future. Not if I fail in this
project. I don't know what my future may be. I'm
afraid some of your neighbors don't understand
reason, and I don't want anyone attached to me,
anyone who could complicate matters."

"They wouldn't be like that, Sam."

"I hope you're right, but I'm not going to let you
involve yourself. After this first spring I may be able
to think about things like that, about staying, maybe.
And with you it would have to be staying, wouldn't
it? There's nothing less permanent here."

He watched a flush come to Meg's cheeks. "If," she
said, her lips trembling, "if I have to, I'll live with it,
Sam. I—" She lost the thread and looked aside, and
Merritt laughed gently and hugged her tight to his
side, sorry that he had to laugh at her, because she
began to cry.

"Meg, Meg, you're just not taught that way, are
you? You couldn't; and I couldn't leave you in the

mess I'd make for you with your neighbors. Come on, be sensible."

"I'd go with you, Sam, wherever you went."

"You're Hestian," he objected, and realized the tone of it after he had said it, that he had meant it less for her sake than for his: he pictured Meg Burns on a starship, or anywhere but on Hestia, and knew he would have to love her more than he felt capable of loving anything—to spend his life tied to her.

Meg caught his eyes and her own looked deeply hurt; he knew then she understood far more than he had said. She had been willing to take that step across to him, forever; and he had not been, and it was too late now to save her pride or pretend otherwise. She backed out of his embrace and drew a deep breath, pressed her lips together: no hysterics, and he admired her for that.

"You're honest," she said quietly.

"So have you been," he said, and did not know what more to say. Another woman might have walked away from him; Meg simply stood there, civilized, hands folded, trying not to cry.

"I feel too much for you," he said, "to let you be hurt worse than this. Don't hate me, Meg. Don't hate me."

She shook her head slowly. "It's all right," she said, and let go her breath. "It's all right."

"Come on," he said then, and offered her his hand. "Let's go back to the house."

She took his hand, slipped hers again within his arm as they walked as if there were nothing amiss, though she furtively wiped her cheek with the back of her hand, nineteen and with her dream in shambles. He had long leisure to think, of Lilith Courtenay, of himself at twenty-one and now at star-traveled twenty-eight; thought of trying to tell Meg of Lilith and *Adam Jones*, and could not think how to do that without making it seem Meg Burns was beneath that. *Love* was not something he could say and mean with Meg's simplicity; he realized that in the moment and he had never felt so crushed by anyone, the uncovering of a deficiency in himself he had never known. He had come to congratulate himself on his being on Hestia, on his seven years' gift, on his meticulous devotion to farmers who must look up to him, on his dreams for a world, and their gratitude.

And Meg Burns showed him himself.

They came in silence back to the station, and into the gates and within the yard now crowded by a new and makeshift barracks.

And suddenly, halfway to the steps of the house itself, Meg stiffened and turned back to look, her face stricken with alarm.

"Lady, Where's Lady?"

Merritt looked. The dog was nowhere in sight; and he could not remember when or where she had left them.

"She may have gone off across the hill or still be hunting." he said. "Don't worry about her."

"Oh, but she never strays. It's nearly sundown, and she's always back for dinner. She'd never wander off hunting when it's dinnertime."

He hesitated, looking at the shadowing sky and at her. "I know how you love that dog," he said, unable to see her further distressed. "I'll go back and look. Maybe I can find her."

Meg caught his arm as he started to go. "No. No. You know better than to do that. She'll come home on her own, she will. Please don't try."

She was saying it only to stop him; he knew it; and knew it was sense she was trying to prevent him, the most basic of rules of her life. He stopped, gave up the gesture. "I'm sorry," he said abjectly. "Meg, I'm sorry."

"She's not lost," Meg said, and assumed a cheerful confidence like putting on new clothes. "Come on, come on; she'll make it home without our help. Let's get out of the cold."

"I'll tell you how it's going to happen." Porter's fist slammed down on the table between them so that the dishes rattled. "You're going to get started this week, Mr Merritt. We've got men sitting idle out there. You're not putting us off till next summer or next winter."

"I'm not satisfied—"

"Well, I am. And so are the people downriver. Just how many of us are you prepared to argue with? My men came out there today ready to work, and they'll be there again tomorrow, and we expect to start, Mr Engineer."

"Whatever we do up here, those families downriver had better get to high ground by spring, and that's the plain and hard truth. We've started cutting timber; we can start the diversion flume so we can work there, but I'm not ready yet to commit all our supplies and that number of lives on the site without more study on the far side of the river. You say we're running out of time. I'm telling you it's going to be a slower process all along than you think. I'm not satisfied we have time enough this season. If you insist on going ahead against my advice, I won't be responsible."

"You're going to be responsible, Mr Merritt," said Porter, "because if those plans are faulty, you've been wasting our time. And you'd better hope you're some good, because if you're not, people downriver are going to get killed; and if people get killed, I very much doubt you're going to pick up your baggage and just walk away. Don't count on it."

"I'm not going to be pushed."

"You'll take your chances in the valley same as us. If we go under, so do you, so think again, Mr Merritt."

"Tom," said Frank Burns, "I don't think this is accomplishing anything. —Mr Merritt, I promise you we're not trying to be unreasonable, but we're trying to make you see we'd rather take the chance. We're on the brink of starvation on some farms—not all, not all; and we aren't feeling the pinch yet, but we will if there's another disaster like last spring. We're remembering that: starving men can't work; and we're not willing to see another fifteen families go down the river while we sit waiting. Now, if you can show there's danger, well, we'll advise people to go to high ground right now, in case we fail. The one thing you can't ask us is to sit and do nothing."

"If we waste our supplies in a false effort—"

"Everything on Hestia is limited; our land is limited. Tom's right: we haven't got the time for you to be sure as you'd like."

Merritt cast a glance at Amos Selby, questioning;

and the riverman gave a slight lift of the brows and shrugged and looked at the table.

"Amos," Merritt insisted.

"Well," said Amos, "I tell you this: I got faith in your good sense, Sam, but I also know what's going to wash down on us come spring, and I couldn't choose."

"*We* got the people," said Porter, "and we know what we choose to do. You haven't got any choice, Merritt. None."

Merritt pushed back from the table and looked at them and down the length of it, at all the silent faces, and at the women and children who stood silent in the room. Then he turned and started for the stairs.

"*Merritt!*" Porter shouted at him; and when he failed to turn in that selfsame instant, a man left the end of the table to block the stairway.

Merritt turned about then and looked at Porter, unhurriedly.

"If you have some idea about destroying the plans," said Porter, "you'd better think again. —Vance, you get upstairs and see what you can find in his papers."

"Wait a minute now," said Amos, leaving his chair. "I don't think that's called for."

"Not in my house, no," said Burns. "I think Mr Merritt appreciates the desperate feeling our people have—isn't it so, Mr Merritt? I can't think you'd be so reckless."

Merritt let go his breath slowly. "You'll remember later it's against my advice we're going ahead. I'll tell you about it."

"We're content with that," said Porter, "so long as we get started. I've waited too long for Earthmen to make up their minds. You people never settle on an answer you like, no, not for fifty years, while people and their stock are drowning. You people are used to sitting where it's safe and making theories because you got leisure for it. Well, I've had enough waiting. So has everyone else on Hestia; and I suggest those plans had better work, Mr Merritt."

"If they don't," said Merritt, "you can get together and draw up some of your own. —Move your man, Porter, I'm going upstairs."

Porter said nothing, but Burns gave him a hard look and Porter finally gave a jerk of his hand that removed his kinsman from the stairway.

One of the cattle lowed, a sound out of place in the middle of the night; and Merritt turned over in bed, restless with the upset in the house. The sound worried at him; he kept an ear attuned for several dim minutes after, somewhere between sleep and waking, not sure he had heard it or how worth an alarm it was: his credit was low enough in the house.

Then there was a general stirring in the pens, sure sign that something was amiss in the yard. Merritt hurled himself clear of the covers and started dressing. One of the dogs barked furiously, then yelped into silence.

"Wake up!" Merritt yelled down the hall, and slipped his other foot into his boot and started running, himself and one of Porter's men at the head of the stairs before the alarm was even sounded. Folk were stirring out from all sides; and by now the barracks outside must be alerted: there was shouting from outside.

And other sounds: the splintering of wood, heavy bodies moving as some of the cattle broke free, bawling in panic. Lights flared inside: torches and lanterns lit from the hearth. Children huddled in stifled panic at their mothers' sides.

"Watch that door," Burns ordered. "Sam Merritt— you got that outsider gun of yours?"

"Here," Merritt called back, pushing his way to the fore. "I'll take the yard if I've got some help."

Three men volunteered and pushed after him; and others slipped the bar on the front door and let them out into the bare-earth yard, within the walls.

Lights were on in the slit-windowed barracks: no one there was opening doors. The heavy-bodied shapes of several cattle huddled in a corner of the wall, then with the unpredictability of herd beasts, darted in wild panic to open space, dodging in confusion about them, a rush of hooves in the dark. Merritt stepped out when it was over, scanned the shadows and the rim of the wall for intruders, and saw nothing.

"Come on," he said to his companions, and led the way around the corner to the back of the house, where the cattle pens were.

Sheep were loose too, cornered and climbing over one another as if they hoped to scale the wall in that corner of the irregular yard; and there were dead ones and dead cattle on the ground, and the black dog too, like a puddle of shadow on the dirt.

"Throats were cut," said one of the men who had knelt to inspect a dead sheep.

Voices broke forth behind them, doors open from

the main house and the barracks, men coming out armed, bringing torches and lanterns.

And the light fell on a dark shape head-high in the center of the vacated sheepfold: a black thing on a pole, upright in the earth. Merritt seized a lantern from a man near him and advanced to inspect the object, then with an oath struck the pole down. Lady's head rolled free of the stake, staring sightlessly into the darkness.

"It's one of the dogs," someone said. "How'd they do that so quiet?"

There was a rising note of panic in the voice. Merritt rounded on it. "She was missing this evening," he said quickly. "Keep it down. Keep your eyes open. We don't know we're not being watched right now."

"But why the dog—like this? Why go to all that trouble?"

"I'd guess," said someone else, a deeper voice, that carried, "that it was a warning that don't need much translation. The dog's a human animal. It's the dogs they hate most."

"Get a shovel," said Merritt. "No need for the kids to see this. We'll salvage the sheep and the cattle— drag the carcasses out of the way so we can get the others back into the pens."

The doors to the main house were letting out a flood of others now: the voices of women were among them. Merritt left the men at work for a moment and went back to head them off; Meg was there with her father, and most of all he did not want that.

"How many did we lose?" Burns asked.

"About half a dozen," Merritt said, and took Meg's

arm in a hard grip. "Get the kids back inside, will you? It's a mess out here."

"I heard a dog bark once. Did Lady—?"

He hesitated on a lie, thought of Meg waiting and waiting for the animal. "She's dead, Meg. Both the dogs, I'm afraid. I'm sorry."

She made one sudden start of tears that she quickly gulped under control; but she did not try to go to see. He was glad of that.

"Get inside," he asked of her, and when she was gone he looked at Burns, and at Porter, who had joined them.

"They've never passed the gate before," said Burns.

"Whatever they are," said Merritt, and his own hands were shaking, "it was a bladed weapon that did that damage; and they're men enough to use tools and symbols."

"We knew they'd come when men started gathering here in numbers," said Porter, "and when trees started falling. I'm afraid it's the start, not the final blow. You wanted a convincing reason why we can't wait, Merritt. I don't think I need to explain this one."

6

"Just about clear, Mr Merritt."

Merritt looked from the chasm to the young work-man-farmer—George Andrews, from one of the smaller farms—and drew back a little from the edge.

"All right," he said, handing Andrews the checklist. "George, when everyone is clear, when you've personally cleared every name on this list with a live body, give me the signal."

"Yes, sir."

Andrews was off at a run, for they were behind schedule in the day—and took his post at the suspension bridge, shouting and cursing the men crossing it to greater speed, to clear the vast cliff that was going to lose a goodly portion of its face. It was the biggest blast they had yet touched off, waiting in that opposing face, and it would yield them rock enough to make a real foundation in the riverbed. It was the beginning.

"Hey, there," Amos Selby's voice, when Amos was not supposed to be there. Merritt turned and saw the riverman and his son, held out his hand with a grin.

"Did you come to watch the big blast?"

"If you're going to mess up my river," said Amos,

"I'm going to have a look at what you're doing. —Are we just about in time?"

"You're supposed to be late, as it happens; but they cross that bridge as if they had all day."

"Huh. Us Hestians ain't made to love heights, flying or otherwise. You wouldn't get me out on that bridge, no, sir."

"Hasn't broken yet," said Merritt.

Amos eyed the fragile rope structure with an expression of distaste. "What surprises me is the People haven't got past you yet to cut it."

"That's what those little sheds are at either end: guard posts. We've heard things skulking about here these last two weeks, but they haven't had the nerve to try anything. —How do things stand downriver? Did you bring us some more men?"

"About thirty-nine this last trip—more going to walk up. Makes a proper city you got growing back there at the station now."

"And a road between here and there. Don't forget that; besides us changing the course of your river for you."

"Couldn't fail to notice. The place is looking more civilized than New Hope already. Can't imagine what it's going to look like with a small ocean where Upriver used to be."

"We'll be doing more building on the dam than on the fortifications from here on out. You watch that cliff in a few moments. —Hey, Ed, get the Selbys some headgear. —And you two wear it, hear? No telling when something's coming down on you around this place. We're about ready to blast."

"I want to see this," said Jim. "Is it safe to stand out here?"

"Ought to be, ought to be. First time I've ever managed something like this, I'm obliged to tell you. Motherworld ways are different."

He saw Andrews' signal, and the bridge was clear. He waved back and then left the Selbys to attend to business.

It had needed a great deal of planning and argument with the haste-minded Porters to determine where to set that charge, and at last it all came down to the touch of a switch on this side of the river. Part of the cliff face bellied out and fragmented while the belated sound reached them, and the ruin settled slowly down again, waiting to be moved by wagons. Great trees—an entire earth bank from higher up—turned loose and became part of the slide, vanishing into the dust before the echoes died up and down the canyon.

When everything was at rest again, Jim Selby gave a long quiet whistle, and Merritt, who had not realized he had been holding his breath overlong, let it go and relaxed. The men knew it was right, and cheered; the experience of smaller blasts let them know what this should have done—and it had: their long work had paid off.

Merritt stepped to the safe planking and let go of the suspension cables, Jim and Amos behind him. The Miller cousins came with them, to take up stations in the farside guardpost, abandoned during the blast— three of the best shots in the high river, the Millers, and armed with the best guns: the farside guard station was the most dangerous, the most exposed, where a severed bridge cable could isolate them for a night or longer. No matter that the post had never been seriously threatened: standing three days at the farside station equalled guard service for a whole week otherside, and entitled the guards to the other four days in the main house back at the station, in real beds, in warmth. Even that bribery did not produce many volunteers.

They stopped at the doorway to the guardpost, on the shallow porch. "Sure changed the landscape, didn't it?" Dan Miller observed, leaning on his rifle and gazing out hillward. Merritt nodded. There was nothing left but yellow powder and great boulders and splintered trees, where a tall cliff had stood.

"I'm going to have a closer look," Merritt said. "I won't be long and I won't go out of sight. You can watch from here—no need us all taking chances."

"Yes, sir," said Dan Miller; but Jim made a gesture to his father, who shrugged and leaned against the shed, and Jim evidently meant to come.

"Stay to my tracks," Merritt advised him, but he was not sorry to have the company. There was a loneliness about farside that prickled the back of the neck, even by noonday, even with the noise of the blast still echoing in the senses. There was a silence here, that all men's efforts had not yet shattered.

Pebbles rattled and rolled down underfoot. The sound of the river reached them distantly. Merritt gave his attention to the path that rimmed the slide area downslope, Jim's shadow close behind his on the sun-baked earth: it was a day like the season, with an icy wind and yet with sun-heat enough to warm a man overmuch on the climb.

A steep climb up hardened-mud steps put them on the security of the upper bank, where no earth had been loosened; and from that vantage it was possible to see all the scope of the canyon and the man-scarred otherside.

"Man," Jim breathed. "I've seen folk try to dam the river before, but they never went at it on this scale. You sure got things going when you decide to move."

"Question is," said Merritt, "whether even that's fast enough. Porter's been yelling about the time we've spent building roads and guard posts; but at least we haven't lost a man yet. Well, Harkness, but—"

"That wasn't on the job."

"No. But I don't intend any more accidents."

Jim looked about him, and grimaced into the sun that was in their faces from the height, back to the east and the Upriver. "You know," he said, "I never thought of it, but I guess the station is the first holding on Hestia that's covered two sides of the river at once. This has never been ours: but it is now."

"So far undisputed—but I'm afraid that won't last."

They walked the ridge westerly, where a gap in rocks and trees afforded a single glimpse of the promontory of Burns' Station, a lonely outpost against all the wilderness about them; and then they walked back again, to look over the damage to the east slope, as close to that slide as they dared come.

"Looks stable enough," Merritt said, thinking of the workmen and wagons that must pull at the edge of it, and reckoning in this too, he would have Porter at his back.

Something rattled away downslope, a rock out of place; and it would have sounded like some belated settling, but that it was followed by a frantic scrabbling. He centered on the source of it, walked higher with Jim trailing after him.

Suddenly a brown form moved among the rocks, scrambled to climb and slid back with a shifting of powder, scuttled sideways and hit worse, plummeted down in an awesome slide, dislodging dust and abrading rock.

"We got one," Jim said at his shoulder. "The blast— must have caught it."

Merritt started running along the ridge in that direction, picked out a way with his eye as he stopped. Jim caught his arm, objecting silently; he shook off the warning and started down, concentrating on his steps. A rattle of stone behind him advised him Jim was with him.

"Stay put," Merritt said. "If I slip I'll need help."

Jim stopped then; Merritt kept walking, slowly, settling rocks into place with his feet, not looking at his goal, but at the ground he had to walk, until he was almost on it.

The golden body lay with feet downhill, of one tone with the earth and the rocks, but silver down covered it: unconscious, unmoving . . . ribs and belly gave with breathing.

And female. Merritt approached it carefully, not least for the hazard of the slide . . . a woman-sized, fragile shape, long-limbed. The downy skin was torn and bloodied; the hair that thickened and closely capped the elongate skull was likewise touched with blood at the temple. Merritt bent and gingerly touched the long-fingered hand that was so nearly and so much not—human, saw the feet, long-toed, of that sort that had left prints the night the boat was set adrift. The face was humanlike: long eyes, closed, with silver lashes and faint silver brows; a short, flat nose; a thin, wide mouth—prognathic features, jaw farther forward than human, but delicate; the body was thin and wiry, the breasts hardly more than a child's, but the face gave the impression of a little more age.

Merritt considered a moment, with pebbles sifting downslope from under his braced feet and knee. He was anxious to move her, for it was no place to linger; but she was no human woman, and there was likely impressive strength in those slender limbs, like an animal's. He hesitated to take that awesomely alien thing into his arms, next his throat, but he detected no sign of consciousness, and finally with great tenderness of her injuries, he lifted her to him and rose. She was surprisingly heavy, limp muscle, like a relaxed cat. He walked the slide slowly, sweating with exertion and with caution, and finally had Jim's hand gripping his sleeve, drawing him up to solid ground. He let her down then on the ridge, at Jim's feet.

"I'd never seen one," Jim said in awe, dropping to his knees, and a flush came to his young face. "Sam, she's just about human, isn't she?"

"Just about." Merritt hesitated, then felt up and down the fragile limbs and body for broken bones. There were none that he could tell, and under the

touch of his hands the being stirred, lips parted—
teeth not quite human either. The canines were well-
developed. Merritt drew back his hand quickly,
chilled to the depth of him.

Brown eyes, almost all pupil, came open and wid-
ened, and with a spitting snarl the being came up
and tried to bolt. Merritt seized her, and it was like
taking rash hold of a frenzied animal: she twisted
and fought so that it seemed she must dislocate
something, and when he grappled for a better hold
she fastened her sharp little teeth into his hand and
held like death itself.

"Get her!" he shouted at Jim, for the bite was like
to crush bone and he could not break it; and there
were several frantic moments on the ridge while he
and Jim together worked to subdue the being. She
fought them so long as she had a hand or a foot free,
and it needed both of them using both weight and
strength to restrain that twisting body short of strik-
ing her senseless.

Merritt took his belt and secured her hands, and
Jim's about her ankles reduced her to stoical submis-
sion. She only lay panting for breath and staring off
into the hills, while Merritt and Jim stood back and
inspected their own wounds. They were all smeared
equally with her blood and theirs, and for comment
Jim only looked at Merritt and shook his head in
wonder.

"There can't be much wrong with her, at least,"
Merritt said, pressing out the purpling wound in his
hand. It was deep and exceedingly painful. "I'm glad
she went for the hand first, and not my throat."

"I guess she's scared out of her mind." said Jim,

and bent down and reached out for her shoulder. She snapped at him like a dog, but when he persisted and stroked her head as if she were an injured animal, she endured that harmless attention, though without pleasure. She began to shiver.

"What are we going to do with her?" Jim asked.

"I don't know," Merritt confessed. He knelt on the other side of her and she jerked about to look at him. Her strange eyes had gone brown now instead of black with hysteria. No white showed at all, just the iris, brown flecked with amber. They were not human eyes, but they were beautiful.

"Listen," he said to the creature, and held out his hand just outside the reach of a bite. "Listen, we're not going to hurt you, we don't want to hurt you, all right? You stay still. That's right."

He touched her shoulder as Jim had, and turned her over and picked her up, holding her tightly so she could not get at his throat. She could have made carrying her impossible; she did not. She tensed only while he rose, and then gave a little against him, still not quite relaxed, but not resisting either. He kept a tight grip on her arm, not letting her face toward him where he could help it.

"Are we taking her back to the house?" Jim asked incredulously. "Sam, they'll just kill her."

"No, they won't," he said.

It was impossible even to cross the bridge without attracting a crowd at the other end; by the time they had come as far as the courtyard of the main house, the news had preceded them, and there was a gath-

ering of every man off duty and of all the household
too.

Merritt found it impossible to force a way with all
of them pressing in to see, every man of them at once
curious and loathing their long-time enemies, the
night-terror brought into plain daylight, restrained
and helpless.

He had to set the creature down finally, amid the
courtyard halfway to the house ... let her rest her
weight on her bound feet and balance against him.
All the faces crowded in on her were too much. She
turned her face against his chest and rested there,
trembling.

Frank Burns arrived, the crowd breaking to let
him through, and he stared in disbelief at what gift
he had brought them; Hannah came out too, drying
her hands on her apron as she came.

"I didn't believe it," said Burns finally. "How did
you catch her?"

"She got into the blast area," said Merritt, "and I
need a place right now to put her."

"Not in my house," said Hannah Burns, who was
the soul of hospitality to everyone; and when Merritt
gave her a look of disappointment she gave a quick
sigh and a distressed shake of her head. "Sam Merritt, you expect me to take *that* in? Look what she's
done to you. Look at you."

"We have the chance now to find out what these
beings are and how they think. I need a place to put
her where she can't get loose, maybe one of the
storehouses—"

"There's a supply room upstairs," said Burns. "Next
the closet. You know it."

"Thanks," said Merritt, and picked up his burden again, swung her sideways to take her through the curious bystanders, carried her up the steps and into the main house.

She screamed, fought, brought into that shadow. She gave a great heave that almost flung her out of his arms, and he would have dropped her, but that Jim quickly seized her feet. She continued to struggle until they had to throw her face down on one of the tables and hold her, but at last she seemed to realize it was hopeless. She lay quietly, breathing with the rapidity of hysteria, and Merritt relaxed his grip carefully, still keeping his hand on the small of her back lest she throw herself off the table and hurt herself. She did not move.

When he looked up, he saw Meg watching him from the foot of the stairs; and without conscious decision he drew his hand from the creature's warm skin. Meg crossed the room to look at the prisoner, stopped a few paces away and studied it, moving around to have view of its face, her own expression apprehensive: apprehension became alarm as the creature gave a sudden heave and almost came off the table. But for Jim's intervention, it would have fallen, and it would not rest satisfied until it had worked into a position in Jim's hands from which it could watch the both of them.

"It's female," Meg said with a frown of surprise, and stared at it uncomfortably where it half-lay against Jim. "I saw it from the window; I couldn't believe you'd bring it into the house. What do you intend with it, Sam?"

"To learn." He took the strap about the creature's

ankles, worked it free: it had cut cruelly. The creature sat very still, only drawing her feet up when he had freed them.

"Meg," he said, "is there some water hot? I'd like to clean her up. There's dirt in those scrapes."

Meg sniffed, and nodded.

The creature did not like being bathed, not in the least; and shivered and trembled all through the process of washing her injuries, shaking water all over Hannah Burns' downstairs floor, and all the dining tables. She resisted the more when Meg tried to wrap her in a sheet, indignant and frightened at once. Merritt saw the reaction and took it off her.

"Don't try," he advised Meg. "She doesn't understand what you're doing."

Meg stared at him and at the prisoner, clearly distressed for the creature's nakedness; and there had been a somewhat similar look among the men about the yard, a guilty look for their thoughts: Merritt recognized it finally. Hestians were not accustomed to such freedoms: in their cold climate, that was only natural. But this golden creature was provided by nature with a considerable body heat and a coating of down that was more apparent to the touch than to sight, save in sunlight. Quite probably it would find the room heat stifling, and the sheet more so.

"I wonder," said Jim, "what she must be thinking. She can't understand much of buildings and people."

"She's probably thinking," said Meg, "that she'd like to kill us all and she's going to be delighted to get the chance. I don't think she's afraid of punish-

ment any more than a wild animal is. She just wants
a chance at us."

Merritt ignored the warning, nodded to Jim. One
on a side, they drew the creature up the stairs,
holding tightly when she balked, letting her walk.
He opened the storeroom and found it empty, a mere
closet with a slit for a window: not even the creature's
slim body could pass that.

And when it knew that they were going to force it
into that dismal hole, it let out a moaning whimper
and shrank back, pressed its face as far as it could
against Merritt and shivered.

"Poor thing," said Jim, "she's not going to like this,
not at all, but what else can we do with her?"

"Get her hands loose; I'll hold her. She may take
the room apart, but we can't leave her tied up in
there."

She stood still for that, so far as it went, but
predictably she tried to bolt. Merritt had a strong
grip on her this time, and her strength, near
exhausted, was quickly spent. She quit fighting and
stared at them, dark-eyed with hate or fright, or both.
A tear traced its way down her cheek.

Once inside, she gave a sudden wrench and freed
herself by surprise, drawing back into the niche
formed by the empty shelves and the corner. Merritt
stood back, not threatening her or offering to restrict
her movement, and after a moment she relaxed and
peered toward the window. Then her eyes darted back
to him as if she expected a surprise attack.

"It's all right," he said gently.

She shivered, backed all the way to the corner and
sank down in a little knot. The long-fingered hands

covered her eyes, her shoulders giving once or twice as if to sobs, but there was no sound.

"You should have shot it," said Porter, in the conference that had gathered unbidden in the main hall. Merritt glared at him.

"I have leave to do what I want and ask what I want so long as it contributes to the work here," Merritt said, "and in my opinion, what we could learn from one of her kind is of value."

"And what she'll draw here is trouble," said Porter, to which no few of the others muttered agreement.

"The trouble is already here," said Merritt. "Better to understand it. She'll bother none of you where she is. Let be.

"I say we get rid of her now," said one of the Porter cousins. "Send her back like we got the dog back."

"I said no," said Merritt, "and that's the end of it."

"You don't understand," said Porter. "You don't know them. We do."

"No argument, Porter. So long as I'm doing my job and hurting none of you, I won't be argued with. I don't think I'm unreasonable."

There was an outcry at that, and Frank Burns put his considerable bulk at Merritt's side.

"Look here," Burns said, "I don't like sheltering one of them, but I don't think Sam Merritt's that much wrong. After a hundred years here, we still don't know what these creatures are; and if it's his craziness, it's not hurting any of us here so far. He's done a good job up to now and worked himself double-shifts often as not, and I don't see any reason to come to blows over this. We got too far to go to find us another engineer; and there's nothing wrong with the one we got. So you let him be while you're on my land; and think it over: you owe him better than this."

"You're right you do," said Amos Selby, from another side of the room. "I don't like the People none either, but Sam's asked blessed little of us till now. You're right he's an outsider and he don't understand much how we feel in some things, but he's not prone to try to push us into things. I figure he's due the same patience, even when he's wrong, like some of us have been when he's been right. What harm's that one little creature doing us locked away up there?"

"And what if she gets loose and kills one of us in our sleep?"

"I'll see she doesn't," said Merritt. "I'll take the responsibility for keeping her secure; no one else has to worry for that."

"We can manage," said Burns; and still complaining, but more softly, the men filtered out of the room, Porter with them. Merritt gave Amos Selby and the Burnses a grateful and inclusive look.

"It's all right for now," said Burns, "but I hope you know what's going to happen if something does go wrong, or if she gets loose and hurts somebody."

"It's certain," said Meg from her mother's side, "you can't keep her shut up in that little closet—just for practical reasons, which I'm sure you can think of, Sam. You'd do a lot better just to turn her out."

Merritt frowned, unhappy that Meg did not stand with him. "No. Maybe we can't manage without some rearranging of things up there, but—"

"We're not set up to play jailers," said Burns. "We

haven't the facilities at all. You see what kind of problem this is."

"It's certain she'll slip any restraint," said Meg.

"Iron . . . she can't get free of," Merritt said. "I don't like to do that, but if it's that or shoot her—"

"She'll tear herself to pieces against a chain," said Amos. "It'd be kinder to shoot her, Sam."

The argument was over. The creature's staccato screams suddenly hushed as Merritt snapped the leather-cushioned iron about her ankle and finished the permanent closing. Jim was holding her, arms tight about her from behind, but she was no longer fighting. When Jim let her go she sat down in the floor and jerked and clawed at the metal ring, then seized the chain in her hands and tried to pull it out of Merritt's grip, rising as she did so. The great brown eyes were brown only around the rims now, the nostrils of her flat nose flared wide; and there was a sudden shift in her look, from panic to the wildness before attack. Merritt saw it coming, jerked hard on the chain and spilled her to the floor.

It needed both of them holding her even so to carry her down the hall and into her new quarters, a dilapidated guest-room with a wider window; and her shrieks of rage filled the house and must be audible all the way out in the yard. Only when she realized that she was in a wider, lighter room she calmed a little, and they let her go.

She walked about the floor and up to the window, while Merritt secured the other end of the chain permanently with bolts—took up on it so that she could not quite reach the window to touch it. And every time she stopped and the chain would drag she gave a little shake of her foot, and at last sat down disconsolately and pulled at it.

"I'm sorry," said Merritt gently, and pocketed his tools, stood up. From the plate on the table he offered her an apple: it was said the People liked that human import and stole fruit from orchards.

He came too close, bending down again. The long-fingered hand slapped at his so fast it stung and the apple rolled from his fingers to the floor. But then she only stared at him, hurt, warning him with her eyes to come no farther.

"All right," he said gently. "All right."

He rose again and backed away to the door where Jim stood. She stared at them, darkeyed—furtively her hand reached for the apple and long fingers curved about it as she gathered it back to her stomach.

"*Ithn,*" she said plaintively; it was voiced, not a whine or a snarl. "*Qu'ii oi.*"

"Is that talking?" Jim wondered, and Merritt came forward again and knelt down in front of her, offered his hand, though at a safe distance.

"Come here," he said. "Come here."

"*K'irr,*" the high-pitched voice echoed. Merritt turned his hand palm up, offered it more plainly. She edged back, then leaned forward nervously and set the apple on the floor within his reach—retreated again with arms clasped round herself.

"I don't want it back." he said, and rolled it toward her. She took it and polished the dust off it, kept it in both her hands, bewilderment in her large eyes.

"Hey," said Jim, also bending down to put himself

on her level. "Hey there—you do understand a little, don't you?"

"*Eh*," she said, short and sharp. "*Eh*."

"You," Merritt said, and she echoed that sound too, but with a slightly different tone.

"I think she's trying to say things back," said Jim, "but I don't think she can make it."

Merritt tapped his chest several times, the age-old gesture. "Sam," he said.

"*Ssam*," she answered; and then if there had been any doubt of her understanding, touched herself. "Sazhje."

"Sazhje," he echoed, pointing at her. "Sazhje?"

She tapped herself affirmatively. "Sazhje." And then she spread her hands and reached out, jerked at the chain, spread her hands again. That did not need translation. Merritt shook his head sadly, but that was a human gesture and she did not appear to understand. She jerked at the chain more violently, uttering short piercing cries, and fought it with a concentration that made Merritt doubt her intelligence anew. He saw she was hurting herself and instinctively reached out his hand to stop her.

She bit him hard, not letting go; and in desperation he cuffed her on the side of the head so that she turned loose. In the look she returned him there was not a bit of civilization or penitence. His hand was bleeding anew, new bites beside the old. He wiped it on his leg and stood up, backing away; and Sazhje, still watching him with feral satisfaction, put the apple to her lips and bit.

7

The site was much changed now that the line across
the canyon floor had begun to grow upward, the rock
face on the far side beginning to diminish considerably, so that more blasting was going to be required
a little farther from the rim this time, the rock
transported down a winding trail on the far side by
labor of men and oxcarts and sledges: maddeningly
slow progress, this primitive chipping away at the
rock, while the winter's lessened flow poured from its
bed to the timber flume and cascaded back to its
original channel.

"We're going to need more men on these crews in a
few days," Merritt said to Porter as they watched the
first of the men head out toward the suspension
bridge for the day's work. "We have to lengthen shifts
if we can't. We're not making progress as fast as we
have to."

"I'm glad to see that bothers you."

Merritt's glance was instant and sharp; he found
Porter's expression what he had thought.

"I mean it," said Porter. "Since you have other
things on your mind—" He gestured down at Merritt's hand, that was bearing another bandage this
morning. "She give you trouble again, eh?"

Merritt only stared at him, and that was not the reaction Porter had evidently wanted. The big man perceptibly revised his line of assault.

"What I mean to say," said Porter, "is that I hope you aren't coming to consider that creature's welfare ahead of ours."

"How should I?"

"I don't know what reasons you may have found."

"Maybe you'd better put what you're thinking in plain words so we both know what you're talking about."

"All right, it's this: we know you never liked this site. And, Mr Merritt, it's a source of wonder to me why you keep on with this creature—sitting in that room late at night, keeping company with it, talking about communication with it. I wonder just what you have to communicate, hey? Or what the whole human race has to say to them, for that matter." He waved his hand toward the east, where the valley showed dark with forest. "That dam's going to make one big lake up there, and it's a case of her kind or ours. I don't think we have anything to communicate about, if they had the brain to do it, which they don't. I hope you aren't having second thoughts about the project. *That's* what I mean. That's what a lot of folks are wondering."

"No, Mr Porter. I know well enough what we have at stake. I understand there's no choice."

"So why do you keep on with her?"

"Because I'm curious. Isn't that my business, Mr Porter?"

"And the fact that it's female has nothing to do with it, of course."

"You want to state that a little clearer too, Mr Porter?"

"If it was male, would you kill it? Or is it misguided sentiment?"

"No, its being female has nothing to do with it, nothing. The fact is it can—*she* can—think and feel the same as you, the same as a human."

"No, sir, not the same as a human, and that's where you make your mistake. Like trying to turn a cat into a dog, it is: four feet, tail, all the right parts, but all the wrong signals. She'll go for your throat one day you get too friendly, and we'll be less one engineer. I call that an unjustifiable risk."

"So if we turn her loose?"

"One more killer on the loose, that's all. You know what you can do with her."

"I'm not going to get rid of her. She's safe where she is and she's hurting no one."

"We aren't safe so long as she's in that room, a room, what's more, fit for people, while I got men sleeping in barracks. I tell you as plain as I know how, I don't like it. I don't like it under the same roof as I am, screaming out in the night for no reason, snarling and spitting like a wild animal—"

"She's quieter now, if she's been disturbing your sleep."

"Is quieter any reason to believe she's safer? Female or not, there's no reckoning of that so far as I'm concerned. They're all killers, all of them. She'll draw others. I have no doubt of that. And we're vulnerable, real vulnerable, depending on that warehouse, on *Celestine*, on our guardposts out here. Men have tried to fight them before and taken precautions; and still woke up with the house afire or worse."

"I'm not denying there's a danger."

"Then why risk it? What good is it? Merritt—if I didn't know better, I'd suspect there was something more than curiosity on your side."

"You can keep your suspicions to yourself, Mr Porter. The fact is, in my mind she's too close to human; and I don't have to kill her. I don't take murder as a casual option; and murder's what it would be."

"They're another species, not human. Murder isn't the word."

"It is as I see it."

"Then—" Porter gestured again to the Upriver. "That lake's going to commit a lot of murder, isn't it?"

"I'll fight for my own kind when I have to; but not when there's no need. So I'll be selective about my atrocities. Don't worry about your dam. It's going all right. And faster if you get me more men on it."

And on that, he walked off and left Porter standing. Proximity was too great a temptation, and Porter was too necessary. He put the man and his manner out of his mind, and walked down to the edge, where the crews were gathering up their gear and still waiting on those who had to walk the bridge first and inspect the ropes. They were returning finally, along with the farside guards.

He gave a casual wave to the others, but when the guards had reached the near side and caught sight of him, they pushed their way past the waiting men and came directly toward him. The rest crowded behind them to hear.

"We had a bad night," said one of the Burnses, who had been the farside guards. "Mr Merritt, we had plenty of visitors; we could see them plain. We saw them near the ropes, and fired at them—it scattered them, but I think we'd better delay work until we've scoured the area. Don't know what they could have set up for mantraps."

Merritt nodded calmly. "We'll do that, then. You did a good job, or we wouldn't have a bridge this morning. We'll have to double farside guard after this. Did you see any sign of them this morning?"

"Plenty of tracks, no bodies. But we thought we hit one or two. Could be they took the dead ones with them or they could have fallen into the canyon. We'd never recover them then."

"It's getting dangerous out there," the other man said. "Don't mind guarding, but I sure want help at it."

Merritt nodded again. "Whatever it takes. We haven't lost any lives yet and we're not going to. Volunteers, get over the other side and look around, carefully. I'll go with you."

"No, sir," said the elder Burns cousin. "No, sir. We aren't taking chances with you. Don't want our only engineer stumbling into something; we know the land. But won't anybody get much done this morning until we have ourselves a look around."

Sazhje was, as usual, perched on the tabletop. She never had understood the comfort of furniture: although she had a cot and a chair, she never used either, but dragged the bedding to the table and made her nest under it, sleeping there at night and sitting

94

atop it at other times, under whatever logic no one had discovered.

Dinner was a time she seemed to anticipate; and each evening that Jim and Merritt came to bring her food, she would bounce down from her perch and pace excitedly back and forth just out of arm's reach. Of late, she would even venture to take the food from them, snatching and jerking back.

This evening, she reached tentatively to Jim's offering, jerked back, and then took it with a sudden move; but she seemed more at ease in their presence, as if the wariness itself had become a ritual. She sprang up to the table again and sat there eating and watching them until she was almost finished.

"Ssam-Zhim," she pronounced, as she would do sometimes conversationally, and offered them a half-eaten apple. Jim, venturing nipped fingers, took it and took a bite.

"Zhim," she said, took it back when he offered and gravely took another bite. Her smooth brow furrowed as in very deep thought, and on her way to another bite she held it out again. "Ah?"

"Sazhje's apple," said Jim.

"Sazhje ap-ph." The syllables came with difficulty, but they were understandable. She had a few words, intelligible to those who knew her small vocabulary. "Sazhje Zhim-Ssam." And what that was to mean was beyond guessing, but Sazhje came off the table and circled a little out of reach, as if she wanted to come closer, but feared to.

"Come," Merritt said. She knew that word. She ventured within reach, held out her hand to touch

95

his, and then Jim's, then appeared greatly alarmed by her own boldness and retreated again.

"Come," Merritt said again.

Sazhje hesitated, then went to the table where she had left her last piece of fruit, picked it up and brought it to them, offering it with great seriousness. When Jim took it from her, she bent down and tugged at the chain at her ankle, looked up and held out her open hands to them.

"She wants that off so bad," said Jim. "Sam, what's it going to hurt?"

"Her," Merritt said. "No. It stays on."

She looked quite dejected when they did nothing for her request, and she went back to her table and sat down again. Jim went to her, though he was taking a chance and patted her shoulder. She actually preened under that attention, turning her head so that her cheek touched his hand. She chattered something in her own language, if language it was, and looked melancholy.

"You've got a friend," said Merritt.

"Think so. Now watch her turn and take my hand off."

But Sazhje did nothing of the sort. She reached up a spidery arm and patted Jim's shoulder, chittering something unintelligible. She reached as far as his head and touched his hair, apparently curious, tugging very slightly at the curls.

"Zhim," she said, and a smile jerked slightly at her thin lips. "Zhim—Ssam."

It was the first time they had ever drawn a smile from her. Jim recklessly set her down off her table and she tolerated it, then decided apparently that it had not been a hostile move at all. She slipped a little out of reach and regarded them both with a coquettish half-smile and a turn of her head, but then inexplicably went shy again and would not be approached. She hissed at them and bared her teeth.

"She's had enough," said Merritt. "Let's not press her."

Merritt folded the notes back again, left them on the desk and started to undress for bed. It was just as he was starting to take off his boots that he heard a strange sound from down the hall: one of Sazhje's irritation screams, muted, as she had never cared to restrain herself before.

He stood up, listened, heard nothing; but the recollection of testings at the bridge troubled him. On that impulse, he quietly took his gun and opened the door, headed quietly down the lamplit hall without raising an alarm: he had no desire to add to Sazhje's unpopularity by rousing the house unnecessarily.

The door was bolted from the outside as it ought to be: they had seen to that after dinner. He slid back the bolt in utter silence and turned the handle, pushed it open on the darkness within.

Sazhje was as close to the shuttered window as she could reach, a shadow among shadows. As she turned and saw him she gave out a soft chirring and her large eyes caught the light. Twice something bumped at the shingled ledge outside, or at the window itself, and went still.

Merritt stopped; he had too much respect for Sazhje's speed to venture to that window himself. He closed the door on her, rushed for the balcony over the main hall, to shout warning; and Sazhje let out a piercing cry, enough to warn any intruders and rouse the sleeping house before Merritt could call aloud.

The alarm was given outside almost in the same moment; there was a clanging of pans and men were shouting, rushing for weapons. A heavy fist pounded on the front door and a human voice shouted; Merritt pelted downstairs and slid the bar back. Others were coming from all parts of the house half-dressed and fully armed behind him.

It was Andrews at the door, George Andrews, bearing a bloody slash across the face and out of breath, a wild figure in the light from the hearth inside and the torches that were flaring inside and about the yard.

"We got a casualty," Andrews breathed. "The People got to us, sir. Ben Porter's dead, tried to stop something as it was coming away from the house. He and I were on sentry duty. Don't know how it happened or how it got past us in the first place, but—"

"Ben's dead?" Tom Porter shouldered his way to the door and all but collared Andrews. "My cousin's dead?"

"I'm sorry," said Andrews.

"What's the situation now?" asked Burns from another quarter. "Are we clear of them now?"

"Yes, sir," said Andrews. "There was only one of them that we saw. And him only when he jumped Ben. I'm sorry, Mr Porter. I fired at the thing— couldn't hit it. We were both standing guard, and when we heard something—it was just too late. I don't think it even aimed to fight. We were just in its way."

"Randy," Burns directed one of his older nephews, "get out there and supervise things in the yard. Andrews, come on in and let Hannah take a look at that cut."

Andrews came in and Merritt, who was holding the door, looked back toward Porter, expecting him to go out to see to his dead kinsman; but Porter showed no disposition to do so. Porter's eyes met his in that instant.

"I warned you what would happen," Porter said; and it was justified, and no moment to argue with the man, not with a kinsman dead. Merritt ventured no reply, not even to offer ill-timed sympathy.

And Tom Porter turned and walked off toward the rear of the hall.

Merritt was taken off-balance by that retreat, until he thought where else that led; and that second thought sent him after Porter, who hit the stairs at a run, gun in hand.

"*Porter!*" Merritt shouted at him, drawing every eye in the room and freezing everyone into a tableau of shock—everyone but Porter. Merritt charged after him up the stairs, two steps at a time; and Jim Selby came to his senses and ran after him too. Then the others moved.

Porter was at the top, headed down the hall, steps thunderous on the board flooring; he reached Sazhje's room and flung the door wide, gun lifting. Sazhje gave one piercing shriek out of the dark, and Merritt hit Porter in a waist-high rush, skidded with him several lengths farther on the floor, into the doors at the end of the hall.

The gun discharged into a wall, deafening; wood

flew. One of the women screamed and so did Sazhje, everything in slow motion as Merritt grappled for the gun, trying to get it from Porter's hand. It discharged again, where, Merritt could not see. Sazhje's staccato shrieks drowned other sounds.

At last he had a purchase on Porter's arm and one hand clear. He hit the man, repeatedly, and still he clung to the gun.

Others had come upstairs; Jim Selby was into it, trying to help restrain the big man without hurting him, and together they were able to pry the gun from his fingers.

Merritt let Porter up then, stood back at safe distance from him. Porter's red face was congested with temper and madness; and for a moment Merritt braced himself for another attack.

"It's your doing," Porter shouted at him. "I warned you, Merritt, I warned you."

"She's not guilty," said Jim Selby, ignoring his father's attempt to draw him out of it, to bring him back to the others that crowded the stairs. "She had nothing to do with it."

"So long as that creature is in the house none of us are going to sleep safe. My cousin's dead. Ben's dead. I'm warning you—destroy it."

"That creature," said Jim, "is a woman, not an animal, and you keep yourself away from her, Mr Porter. If you hurt her, so help me—"

"If you call that a woman, that's your taste, boy, not mine. Is that it? Well, you could do what you like with your pet till now, but I'm losing no more of my kin for her sake."

"Back down, Porter," said Merritt. "Get out there

with your other cousin that needs you. You'll do some
good there, but none here."

"No," said Jim, his young face white with anger. "If
he wants trouble with me, he's got it."

Porter's eyes went from head to foot of Jim's slim
un-Hestian figure, and back to his face again. "You
save yourself till you're older, boy. —Amos, do something with this bastard kid before I have to."

With a cry of rage Jim threw himself at Porter, and
landed one good blow: Porter's answering one rocked
him back half over the balcony railing, wringing an
outcry from others. Porter started forward again, but
Merritt jerked him about and held his arm.

Porter did not resist him, although he was ready
for it. There was a dark anger in the big man's eyes,
but there was calculation too; in height, at least, and
youth to age, they were evenly matched.

"Go downstairs," Merritt said quietly, as if it were
a request.

Porter went, men moving out of his way and
following him down the stairs. Meg was among them;
she delayed for a cold look at Merritt, a hurt and
ashamed look, and went after Porter. Only Burns and
Amos and Jim were left with him on the balcony.

"However you settle it now," said Burns, "there's
someone hurt."

"Are you telling me to get rid of her?" Merritt
asked.

"No, because I know you'll do what you want to do.
But when we have a man dead out in the yard, I
think you'd better consider again. You'd better think
whether what you're doing is worth what it just cost
us."

And Burns left them, head bowed, walked down the stairs. Amos took Jim by the arm and gave him a push down the hall toward their room; and when Jim delayed, gave him a second shove. Jim cast back an angry look, but he went to the room, slammed the door.

"Sam," said Amos, "I got something to say and I know just one way to say it. Is what Porter says true? You think my boy's overly fond of that female? Is that true?"

"No," Merritt said.

"Well, I don't like it. I don't want my Jim having any part of this, and I'm holding you to answer for it, Sam. I mean that. You keep him away from her."

"Jim's grown; he knows his own mind. Don't ask me to do what you can't. It's impossible to tell him—"

"Listen," Amos hissed at him. "Listen and I'll tell you something. Jim ain't my son, and I think you must have guessed that, if someone ain't told you. And maybe it's his real father's blood that makes him wild like that, that's got his head in the clouds and his imagination always messing with things he oughtn't to touch—but he's my wife's boy, rest her soul, that she got of some outsider before I married her, and I love him anyway—maybe better than I should. But I got sense enough to know him; and I know it's the wild streak in him that could take after that thing in there. It's what would appeal to him. So you do what you want to do about her, friend . . . I can look away from that: you're an outsider and I'm too late to tell you what's right and wrong. But I'm not having you infect my boy with your outsider ways and your outsider morals. Jim's got to live on this

world after you've up and gone your way again; and
don't you be putting things in his head he don't know
how to live with. Don't you teach him that thing's
human, or teach him your right and wrong if you got
any where you come from."

Merritt only stared at him, dismayed to hear that
from Amos; and even Amos looked uncomfortable.

"You're a *good* man," Amos said. "But there's right
and wrong on this world, and I expect my boy to
know it and to live by it. And if you got sense, you
will too."

"Meaning?"

"Don't look guilty, even if you ain't. There's an ugly
thing they're saying about you; and I don't want it to
touch my boy too."

"What are people saying, Amos?"

Amos looked down, jerked his head aside. "That it's
odd, your being seen less and less with Meg Burns
since the time you brought this creature in—*I* know
it ain't true, Sam, but Hestia's got a proverb about
outsider morals, and that's how it is. It's hurting Meg
and it's hurting you and my boy; and the sooner you
get rid of that creature the better."

Merritt said nothing for a moment, did not trust
himself to say anything until he had stopped shaking.
Amos stood his ground, his expression pained but
unyielding.

"So," Merritt said, "but of course you don't believe
it."

"Let's put it this way," said Amos. "If it was true, I
wouldn't care. I've held you a friend in spite of what
you are, not because of. We're plain people, and that's
as plain as it can be said. If it means your going

against me now, all right, but you've got precious few friends left, Sam. You'd better take the advice of the few you've got. If another few things go wrong like this, they'll make it right unpleasant for you. You tell me whether keeping that creature's worth it."

"I don't intend to give in."

"And that hard-headed pride of yours is going to be the end of you someday. I never knew a man so stubborn over so little."

"I don't think it's a little matter. I'll manage this project my way, and I'm sorry for Porter and more sorry for his cousin, but it isn't the first time Sazhje's people have made it over the wall. I don't think it's my fault: I don't believe it."

"You tell me what you're planning to do, Sam—no, you let me guess. You're convinced she's human. And that's behind this."

"Meaning?"

"If it suits you to try to stand their side and ours, maybe that's the way you are. Maybe you're still able to come out to the same conclusion as we are; but most of us ain't going to understand how your mind works, and there's some that came here hating Earthmen in the first place, and you aren't doing yourself any good. What you do to yourself, I can't help. But I swear to you, Sam, if I have to take *Celestine* and pull my boy out of here to get him clear of what they're saying—I'll do it. People already look at Jim and know he's not mine; and know where he came from—and I won't let you finish him. *He* may have his dreams and his wild ideas that don't fit Hestia, but he's a riverside Hestian, for all that, and he always has to be . . . ain't no starship going to take him on, when he can't do more than simple addition and sign his name. Don't you take him and set him against his neighbors. Cut your own throat if you like, but you do it alone, Sam, all by yourself."

"I understand you, then."

"But you don't change your mind about that creature, eh?"

"No. Not about her."

He turned and went back to Sazhje's room, hesitated there. She was crouched in the shadows of the far corner, and covered her face against him, looking between her hands.

"It's Sam, Sazhje," he said, for he thought that she might not know him in the shadow, and she had had terror enough for one night.

"Ssam-Ssam," she said, and rose and came across the room as close to the door as she could reach. Lamplight from the hall glistened on her tear-streaked face. She stretched out her long fingers appealingly, curled them up again and extended them. "Ssam."

"It's all right," he told her quietly, which was the expression he always used when she was alarmed; and he came to her, because he could not shut the door on her when she had had such a fright. Her spidery arms went about him and her head against his chest. She was shivering, those tensile-steel limbs hard and gentle in their embrace, her downy skin hot and sweating as it would when she had been gravely upset. He stroked the silky cap of her hair and ran a finger behind the animal-pointed ears, the skin back there baby-soft and with a little fold, for the ears could move. They did so when she lifted her head to look up into his face, shifted back a little and then up, which was her listening gesture.

"Ssam—Zhim? Zhim?"

"Jim's all right."

"Ah," she said, which was a kind of yes. She looked relieved. "Ssam ahhrht?"

"Sam's all right," he affirmed, and over that bit of conversation on her part he would have been delighted earlier; but it was a moment for thinking.

Amos had told him the truth; he had to believe that, knowing the man. And worse, he had to concede that Porter had some large amount of right on his side too. No matter that Sazhje was blameless; in some part he was to blame, trying to make something different out of her, persisting in believing that humans as well could be changed. There was a time to admit defeat: and when it threatened to break the camp apart, it was time to swallow pride and try to undo what mistake had been made.

He went back to his room and brought back tools, and spread them out on the floor in front of Sazhje. She appeared perturbed by his actions, but not panicked; and when he motioned for her to come to him, she did so.

Quietly, patiently, trying not to let something slip and hurt her, he began to work on the closing of the anklet ring. When she realized what he was doing she began to make small delighted sounds, such as only the offering of food had brought from her before. When she grew too excited and bothered his work, he reached up and caressed the side of her head. She grew still again until he had her free and the metal fell to the floor.

Sazhje took the freed ankle in her hands and rubbed it vigorously; and then she rose sinuously to her feet and spun about several times for joy. She gave a shriek of triumph, hushed by Merritt's warning. Then she came to him and reached out a long arm for his, her prognathic face broken into a fanged smile. "Ssam, Ssam, Ssam," she said. "Sazhje ahhrht."

"That's good, Sazhje. Now be still. Be still. And come."

Those were words she knew and could use herself, at least in symbol; and when he drew her toward the door she began to be very excited. When they came to the balcony and found the lower room full of people, the excitement became alarm.

"It's all right, Sazhje," he told her. He put an arm about her as he started her downstairs, Sazhje walking carefully on this unfamiliar structure.

The gathering downstairs had seen what was coming, and stood back in a hostile semicircle: Andrews, Burns, Porter, Meg, Hannah, among about twenty others.

"What are you doing?" Porter demanded as Merritt and Sazhje reached the main floor.

"I'm doing what you want. I'm turning her loose."

"That's less than what I want," said Porter.

"That's all you're going to get," Merritt answered, though others were agreeing with Porter.

"That one's going to come back someday and cut someone's throat," said Ken Porter, Ben's younger brother. "And we're asking for it if we turn her loose."

"She's never hurt anyone," said Merritt, "and won't, if she's not threatened."

"She'll be back," said Porter, and others said so too,

an ugly murmur of human sound that sent Sazhje as close to Merritt as she could get, her hands tight about his arm.

Merritt read the crowd's mood, and Sazhje's; and forced a passage through them, for no one was anxious to get close to Sazhje. He went out the door and across the yard, through groups of men who stared with no friendlier eyes, and past cattle pens that erupted with bawling panic at the proximity of their old enemy, and up to the gate. There was no need to ask the guards to open, not for Sazhje.

"Sazhje's all right now," he assured her.

"Ssam," she said, and flung thin arms about him for a moment, and then was gone. A shadow flitted in the torchlight near the corner and a moment later slipped over the wall without the least appearance of effort: that, for how much protection the walls had ever been.

It was returning into the main room that he dreaded; and none of those gathered had left, save only Meg ... Meg was not there. He passed under their eyes through absolute silence, as though whatever they had said in his absence was more than they wanted to say to his face. He climbed the stairs and crossed the balcony, pursued by their stares and their silence, and slammed the door to his room behind him.

8

The clouds were back, dismal ceiling over the forest, as yet shedding no precipitation, but there was an unseasonal moisture in the air and uncertainty in the wind.

Merritt looked down into the chasm where water went over the flume at its usual rate and boiled onto the rocks below: rain or snowmelt in the mountains would have swollen that flood considerably. Downriver sandbars showed where fall had seen the river high above them, and the riverboats, half-loaded, still plied the middle of the channel with greatest care.

"If the rains and the melt just hold back," Merritt said to Frank Burns, as they walked back from the edge, "we may make it. But that they should come early—"

"We don't panic yet," said Burns. "Sometimes there's a little warming in mid-winter, a little rain: false spring. But I figure we got at least a month left, maybe two; three, with rare good luck."

Merritt cast a worried glance over his shoulder. "Pray for three. Or get me more men up here."

"Sam," said Burns, "the men who didn't come in the first place or at the second call, didn't come because they have families to protect and property to guard. You've been here long enough to know what it would be for a woman and kids to try to hold a place with no men around, or what you'd have left of your farm if you boarded up and took a month elsewhere."

"We're at the point we need that help, even at cost. We're going to have to call the women to move rock if it comes to it. We're going to blast some more this week, and weather permitting, we're going to be working daylight to dark and maybe beyond that."

"You've been double-shift yourself too often, long since. You're showing the effects of it, and my boys have to chase you off the dangerous jobs. You're not winning anything by it, you know that; other men can do some of your work. You don't have to prove anything to us. You know that, I hope."

Merritt shrugged. "About that, I don't bother; but there's problems on both shifts, that's all, and they have to be answered. Frank, if we have an early spring, it's all over. That's the bitter truth. Somebody better warn those downriver families."

"I don't think it's near winter's end, not yet. The animals are still carrying winter coats, the river's still down, and the sea wind hasn't started yet. Just because it's warming here doesn't affect the high snows."

"Farmer's sense?"

Burns laughed softly. "I know you got no appreciation of our ways, Sam, but we aren't in trouble yet."

"We will be, first rain that hits the high river. That flume won't carry a flood and that dike will hold just long enough to make real trouble."

"I sent word long since that any family that's living

riverside now is risking their lives. They're taking precautions. We know this old river; no offworlder has to tell a Hestian when it's dangerous to stay, no offense."

"None taken."

"You're a pessimist, Sam. Are you really convinced it's not going to hold?"

"I'm convinced it's not the best I could have done, but it's the quickest. Maybe if it holds this year we can use it for a diversion while we build again. *That's* what I hope."

"I've heard about your plans for the next stage; Meg told me. So you're really thinking about staying on."

"I was. I'm stubborn. This is my life's work, maybe all I'll ever amount to, thanks to my youthful stupidity in signing on to come here; and if it takes a year or so to finish it right, well, I might be persuaded; and maybe more things, I don't know. After what it's cost me, what else have I got to look forward to? But it's going to cost you people too. It's going to cost you more than you might want."

"They're paying you plenty already."

"Huh. What good is *that* here?"

"Then what kind of payment are you talking about?"

"Free license—to build, to make projects ... my way."

Burns gave him an under-the-brows look, frowned a little. "Sam, if we all live through this, you can about name your price on any terms. But I wonder what attracts you here."

"It's someplace," he said with finality, brushing

aside the inquiry, and sighed and looked up once more at the darkening sky. "Day crew's going back now. You'd better walk back with them."

"Aren't you coming?"

"I have a matter to check out yet. Go on, Frank. I'll catch up with you. I have my pistol, and I've walked that trail a hundred times alone."

"Not in the dark."

"I'll start back before then."

Burns hesitated, nodded then and walked over to join with the line of men headed back to the station. Merritt went his way to the bridge and slowly across that swinging thread to the other side, to take a last look at the blast site.

It was later than he had planned when he started back, across the bridge again and past the guard station. "Stay the night," one of the men there urged him, but he refused, tired, and unwilling to disturb the crew at the house by the search they would surely make. The sky had deceived him. There was suddenly little light left, the overcast palling the sky to an early night, and the wind that had been too warm now blew with knife-edged cold. He left the station and hurried down the sandy trail at a dog-trot for all that he was tired—dreading most the ravine where a bit of woods remained between the site and the safety of the house, a two-hundred-yard stretch that, in spite of trees cleared back from the path itself, had an unpleasant closeness about it, where the trail necessarily bent and one had the feeling of being shut within the gray-limbed forest from all sides. Here, his steps whispering through the dry leaves, it was almost dark, the light cut off except from overhead.

Something hit the trail ahead and bounced, a small object; and the next one hit him on the chest. He skidded aside, ripped his gun out and thumbed the safety off, swung toward a crash of branches.

"Ssam," said a voice from a slight altitude.

He looked up into the limbs of the nearest tree. It was Sazhje.

"Ahhrht, Ssam?" she inquired.

He remembered the gun in his hand and put it away. Sazhje dropped down from her tree and landed on her feet, peered this way and that as if to ascertain whether he was truly alone.

"Sazhje's all right," he said, and held out his hands.

Her face relaxed into a fanged grin, and she came forward, chattered something at him and slipped her long fingered hands into his.

"Ssam come," she said, tugging at him.

"Where?" And remembering that she could not understand that question: "Sam all right?"

"Ah," she affirmed, and pulled at his hands again, anxious to leave the trail.

Warily he moved with her and entered the shadows of the trees, where it was nearly night indeed. She would have led him farther, but he braced his feet and would not go. She chattered at him angrily.

"No," he said, which she understood. He sat down on a fallen log and she sat down next to him astride it. She jerked several times at his arm, frowning.

"No," he repeated.

She rose up on one knee then and edged close to him, her hand on his shoulder, patting his arm excitedly and trying to tell him something. Her frustration was pathetic.

At last she put a thin arm about his neck and patted his face with gentle fingers that did not feel human—warm despite that she was naked in the chill wind; and too slim to be a woman's.

"Ssam," she mourned into his ear.

"What's wrong with you?" he wondered aloud, and caressed her silky head. It drew a chirr of contentment from her, and she nestled almost into his lap and talked at him senselessly, content to be petted. For a long time he stayed there and talked to her in similar fashion; but the last light was going quickly, and he was anxious for what worry he would be causing at the house.

At last he rose to leave her, and she grew visibly upset, at first pleading and then scolding, and took his arm wth such force that he backed away in alarm, tried to pry her steely fingers loose and began to fear he would have to hurt her to get free.

When he jerked back and laid his hand on his pistol her manner changed entirely: she held out her hands and pleaded with tears in her voice, but he went his way, broke onto the trail and began to run in earnest, fearing treachery. For a time a rustling in the leaves pursued him, but when he had left the ravine and come into the open again it was no longer with him.

He came up the hill still running: lights were lit and the outside gates were closed when he came to the station; and a shout went up as they opened to him. He was relieved to be inside with solid wood booming shut behind him, to be surrounded by human faces and human voices. He was still shaking in the knees as he mounted the steps to the main house and walked in the door.

"Sam!" said Burns with great relief. "We were just about to go out looking for you."

"I know, I know. I'm sorry." He controlled his voice and peeled off his coat, hung it on a peg with the others.

"You've been running," said Hannah Burns.

"Some. I knew I was late and it's cold out there."

"We were dreadful worried.—Here. Meg. Get Sam some hot tea and some stew from the pot, will you?"

There were other men eating too; and Merritt sat down at the side of the table nearest the crackling fire and nodded his thanks as Meg set dinner before him. Others went about their business. Meg settled at the bench beside him and leaned against the table.

"Sam, you just about had all the house looking for you tonight."

"I'm sorry. I said I was sorry."

"You stay out so late—always. You're wearing yourself out. I hate to see how tired you are."

He realized that he had lifted a spoonful of stew and was stupidly staring into it; he let it down into the bowl again. He took the cup instead and drank, and then looked at Meg.

"You look in the sky today?" he asked her. "That's why I stay late."

"Does killing yourself help?"

"Let be, Meg." he said, sharper than he had intended, and was instantly sorry. He reached over and took her hand. "Meg, I am tired. Forget it."

"You were more than tired when you came through that door."

"Let be."

"Did something happen out there?"

He considered a moment, weighed how effective a lie would be with Meg. "Sazhje's back," he said quietly. "But don't tell it."

"You saw her?"

"I talked with her a moment—at least for what little she can say. I don't know what she wanted—only that maybe I crossed that odd little mind of hers today and she waited for me this evening."

"After being gone three weeks?"

"I don't know why she came, or what she wanted. Truthfully."

Meg gave a short and humorless laugh. "Maybe it was you."

"Meg—"

She smiled a little. "I'm sorry, Sam. That was mean."

"You know the truth about what there ever was with her; and I'm sorry it ever touched you. That's the main reason I don't want you to mention Sazhje's coming around this evening. I don't want to start it all over again. I have enough on my mind without that."

"You don't have to explain to me. I know you too well."

"Good or ill?"

Her hand closed on his, tightened. "Enough so you can't lie to me; enough to be sure why you do most things, and to know you're worried sick over the work out there. If you think I'll add to your problems, you're wrong."

It was a true shot, well-aimed. He looked into her

eyes and believed her. "There were things I said some time ago," he said, "that I've daily wished I hadn't. I'm mortally sorry for that, Meg; I wish you could understand me then and now . . . but there are things that must hit too hard to ever completely forget."

"Do you *want* me to forget?" she asked, which was the terrible direct-question manner Meg always had, cutting to the heart of things.

"Do you have to ask like that?"

She smiled one-sidedly and shrugged. "Only when the answer's plain. What was true then still is."

"Less so. Less so. Meg, I'd be off this wretched world at the first chance sometimes; and ten minutes after, I don't know. And I'm less and less sure you couldn't leave it if you had to; but I'm not sure you'd be happy outside it."

"I know what you think," she said.

He started to ask what that was, but there was a stamping and an opening of the front door, and Amos Selby and Jim were there with a great deal of commotion. Meg sprang up to welcome them and to take their wraps; and Amos came over after to take Merritt's offered hand.

"I didn't know you were back," Merritt said. "Or did you just get in?"

"About three hours back," said Amos, stepping over the bench to sit down; Jim took the other side, and Meg sat down next to Amos.

"We've been unloading," said Jim. "We—thanks, Hannah," he interjected as Hannah Burns put a bowl of stew and a cup of tea in front of him. Another woman gave the same to Amos. "We got a lot of

supplies and a few new workers, most of them kids.
And food for the next few weeks, anyway."

"How are things downriver?"

"Not much changed," said Amos, "but it's tight
rations in a few areas. They're willing to suffer to
make sure we eat. Anything so long as they know
we're at work up there and the dam is rising."

"You—" Merritt began to ask further of that.

And then an alarm began ringing. Steps thundered
to the door; the door flew open with a thunderous
crash and Ken Porter filled the doorway. "We got a
fire!" he shouted into the silence.

Benches scattered and men rushed for the doorway,
for the tool storage and shovels, and women shouted
for sacking and buckets. Children began to cry.

"Watch it!" Amos shouted at everyone. "You *know*
what started it."

But no one was paying attention, and he looked at
Merritt.

"Better double the sentries," Merritt said. "Meg—
you and the women lock that front door after us and
be careful what you open it to."

He ran, then, after the rest, snatching his coat that
held his gun; and Amos and Jim were at his heels.

It was a warehouse: it was going fast, the entire
yard lit by the fire that had involved the roof and at
least a portion of the adjoining one. Men were carrying supplies out of it, ignoring the danger of collapse,
for the supplies, the food, were life itself.

Merritt collared several men and sent them to the
guard posts himself, to be sure every point was
covered; and then he seized up a shovel and dropped
it again, for in his fatigue the third warehouse only

then occurred to him. Men had lost the first building, vainly trying to smother the fire with buckets of earth: there was no water on the hill . . . it must be carried up from the river; and stinging smoke and wind scattering the dust made the effort impossible.

"Never mind!" he shouted, running. "Get the supplies out of the other one. The explosives . . . get them out!"

Dazed men dropped shovels and stared, some moving, others wiping at eyes and simply trying to see and breathe. It was very hard to hear over the roar of the wind. Merritt shouted at them again and finally went from one to the other, pushing and shoving them into action; then he went to the door of the third storehouse, blind in the dark and the smoke, trying to locate the boxes of caps and the explosives, trying to remember how many there were in all: fifteen, he thought—two on the site already, the rest, the most part—in the warehouse. Heat numbed the air, deadly heat.

He found the boxes, heaved up a double load, started for the door.

"*Sam!*" Burns' great voice bellowed out of the dark. "You found it?"

"Give me some help," Merritt called back, staggering with what he carried. He looked up as the light of fire showed between the shingles of the roof and swore without breath. "We're afire," he gasped as he struggled past Burns and toward the door.

Men were ready there, relieving him of his burden, taking it far from the fire, gingerly.

"Never mind that stuff," Merritt said of the supplies

they were rescuing. "Get back in here and help us before the whole shed blows."

Burns staggered out again, discharged his load to waiting hands, though there were few enough willing to go into that overheated building. There was no time to argue with them.

Twice more he and Burns each made the trip from the inside to the door, and by this time the roof was showering sparks, fire raining down in a roiling smoke. They worked their way back and forth through the tangle of boxes and sacks, sweating and gasping under that heat-sensitized load.

A last time Merritt handed over the explosives to one of the men waiting, and staggered out free into the clearer air, coughing and wiping his eyes. Then there was a wash of air and pressure and sound too deep to hear.

He was on something hard, and on his face, stripped to the waist, a pain in his upper back that seemed to run through his bones and down his spine. He made a frantic effort to move his hands, but someone leaned on his back and held him down. The pain grew worse and he grayed out briefly.

When the thickness cleared from his senses he was still lying on his face . . . he knew the main room of the house, and Jim Selby was kneeling by him, a gentle hand on his brow.

"Sam?" he kept saying.

"It blew," Merritt murmured thickly, and tried again to move. "It blew, *Frank—It's blown—*"

Jim's steady, hard grip on his arm pulled him back to present time. "Mr Burns was inside. Five others got it too. We don't know what happened. No one knows why he went back in; they saw him clear the doorway, and then he went back in."

"There were some boxes left," Merritt recalled. "We couldn't tell for sure which was—we—Meg. *Where's Meg?*"

"With her mother. Easy, Sam. You took a big sliver of wood in the back and a blow on the head, by the feel of it. Stay down."

"Who else, who else, Jim?"

"Frank Burns: in the building when it blew. George Remington; Len Andrews; we still haven't accounted for Tod Miller and the Hansford brothers; we think they're in there. And we have some injuries, lesser ones—we were afraid you'd die on us. You stay quiet."

"What supplies lost?"

"A lot."

A knee came into Merritt's field of vision, and he turned his head painfully to see Amos Selby.

"I'm all right," he croaked. "Amos—"

"We got the fire stopped," said Amos. "It cost us plenty. We're moving what supplies we got left into the house itself, except the explosives. They want our food, they'll have to get us to get it."

"They might next time." Merritt tried to rise. Jim and Amos stopped him forcibly.

"There's nothing you can do," Jim said.

"How's Meg taking it? And Hannah?"

"They'll be all right; they'll be all right, Sam. Lie still."

"Why did he go back?"

"I don't know. No one could see in there."

"Maybe he thought I didn't make it. Maybe—"

"Keep it quiet. There's not a thing in the world you can do now for anyone. Just stay still till we can get time to move you upstairs."

"I can walk."

"You're not going to."

"There's no time—"

"There's no time to replace you. Stay down and listen. We can get more supplies from downriver. We got that planned already. It'll take some time; it's going to hurt folks some; but this isn't the end of us. Not this time."

"Force—ought to go out and check on the men out at the bridge. If—"

"We'll take care of it, Sam. We'll see to it."

The lower room still showed the scars of the night before, the disarranged tables and benches, the stacks of goods, the reek of smoke. But regular as life itself there was Meg Burns trying to put things to rights, pulling the heavy tables around, moving crates.

Merritt descended as far as the warped tread on the stairs before she heard him and looked up; and she brushed her hands on her coveralls and rushed toward him.

"I'm all right," he said, and continued his way down, holding the rail for steadiness. She waited tensely until he had come to the bottom of the steps and then led him to a bench at the nearest table.

"You oughtn't to be on your feet."

"Where is everyone?"

"Mother's resting. Everyone else is out in the yard trying to clean things up and take inventory of the damage. We—" her voice quavered. "We read the burial service this morning."

"Meg, if only—"

"Don't give me *if only*." She sank down opposite him and rested her head on her hands a moment, then lifted tear-filmed eyes to his. "You were in there with him. You tried."

"Others did too, Meg. And they're dead. They just – " There was nothing to say, nothing that would make it reasonable, even to himself. He shook his head and stared at her helplessly. "I don't know why I'm alive. I didn't know he wasn't behind me, Meg. I didn't know."

She took his hand and curved her fingers about it as if he were the one who needed comfort. "There's no way you could have done more," she said. "Go back upstairs. Go back to bed, Sam. You don't need to be down here."

He shook his head. "I'd better find out what has to be done."

"Leave it to Amos and Mr Porter. They're doing all right for now. Amos is leaving in about an hour, on his way for more supplies. He'll beg or threaten them upriver. It's going to be all right, Sam."

"What about the men at the site? Were they all right?"

"They're fine." She stared at him a moment, thinking, and at last spoke it. "She *was* trying to tell you something, wasn't she? She knew what was going to happen."

Merritt nodded slowly. "I suppose," he said, "that she did."

9

Merritt paused a moment to catch his breath, within view of the dam area, and continued uphill. Andrews saw him first and hurried downhill to meet him, offered his hand to help him. Merritt shook him off and walked beside him up to his usual vantage point.

"It wasn't necessary, sir."

"You know it was," Merritt said shortly, and sat down on a log they had long since dragged up for that purpose. From where he was he had a view of much of the canyon, and of the facing wall in particular. Most of that rock beyond it on the upper slope was supposed to be gone. It was not.

"We have men over there now trying to find out what went wrong," Andrews said.

"It sure didn't do what it was supposed to do," said Merritt.

"Maybe," said a voice from behind him, "it had something to do with the instructions we were given."

Merritt did not need to look around to know it was Tom Porter. The voice was unmistakable. He swung round slowly and carefully, and looked up at the man.

"That's one possibility among others," said Merritt. "I suppose it's a very good one."

Porter had tried for an argument with a witness present. Now he folded his arms and stared down at Merritt. "You think you can do something out here you couldn't do from the house, then? Or have you got any good ideas at the moment?"

Merritt gathered himself to his feet slowly, looked at Andrews. "Go see if there's any news from across the canyon," he said, and George Andrews wisely took himself off in a hurry. Merritt turned with dead calm and looked at Porter, eye to eye.

"Porter, I'm not in the mood to argue with you or anyone else right now. If you want things your way, I'll just walk back to the house and let you settle your own problems. But otherwise, stay out of my way."

"We've wasted a week already, and we look like we're going to lose more than that. I haven't insisted you be out here, knowing well enough you couldn't, but now that you are here—"

"Porter," said Merritt, with as much calm as he could muster, "you don't *insist* anything where I'm concerned. If you think you can finish this project, you go right ahead."

"All right, bad choice of words. But you've been out a week and nothing you've left me has worked. The blast didn't go as planned. Reynolds went down on the slide and near went over the edge; he was lucky to get off with a broken leg. We've had two of the oxen slaughtered last night on the farside and we can't expect to get replacements inside a week. The way you want to build that extension of the road out to the dike isn't working; it caved in and hurt a man. I haven't bothered you with such details. Do you want a further list?"

Merritt drew a long breath and wiped the cold sweat from his face. Not in a communicative mood, he turned from Porter and walked to the rim of the gorge.

"Answers?" Porter prodded him.

Merritt shook his head slowly. "I don't know. Looks as if I misjudged. Or—I don't know. If I'd been here, I'd have taken a last check; maybe someone didn't understand my charts. I'd better go over there and look it over."

"I've got a lot of men standing around idle while you're thinking."

"There's no need of that. Put them to work cutting timber. Do they need instruction for that? And for the other, I don't know yet. I don't know. Best too many not go prodding around until we do know. There could be a charge that didn't go. Could be a lot of things. I'll give you answers after I've had a chance to look around. Just stay clear of me."

Meg was standing in the door when the crew came in at evening, warned, no doubt, by the creaking of the outer gate. There was dinner waiting as it always was. Hannah Burns there to welcome them with hot meals, the other women and the children of the household under her direction.

Merritt lowered himself to table very carefully: the walk back had proven almost too much for him. He let his weight to his elbows, settled, gave Meg a tired smile.

"How did it go?" she asked, pausing in the serving. "We were terribly worried when we heard a second blast go off."

"It was planned. It went the way it should."

"You look terrible."

"I'm all right."

"Surely you're not going back out there tomorrow."

"I fairly well have to. Besides, it's not so hard for most of the day. It's the walking that does for me."

The dinner was stew again: it frequently was, due to the large number of men who must eat at uncertain hours. Merritt looked at what Meg ladled into his bowl, stirred it about, swallowed what of it he could tolerate and then excused himself to go upstairs. One of the Burns lads offered to help him; he waved him off and walked up slowly, reached the safety of his room and shut the door. He would gladly have lain down clothed, but he made himself strip out of the clothing all the same, poured water, washed, eased gingerly into bed.

There was a concentrated misery in his back, between his shoulders, where there was a scarcely healed injury the length of his hand: nothing, for a starship's medical facilities; serious enough as Hestians practiced medicine. More than once since his injury he had thought of *Adam Jones* with longing. To be on Hestia under the best of circumstances was a trial of patience. To be hurt and depending on Hestian medicine, to be reduced to receiving messages by runner, to lie for hours on this sagging feather mattress—was another matter entirely.

He slept finally; he did not know how long, but the last of the wick had burned in the lamp and the room was dark. He recognized the lowing of cattle that had wakened him ... ordinarily sooner than it had; and people were moving about downstairs.

127

Something was scratching at the window, insistently. He rose in the dark, his heart beating hard, and retrieved his gun from the table ... padded to the window and listened, hardly breathing. When the sound did not repeat itself, he rapped the gun barrel on the window.

"Ssam," came a hiss from the other side.

He unbarred the inner shutter with his left hand, hurrying, for fear the sentries might spot her and fire. When he flung the shutters inward, there was Sazhje's anxious face the other side of the cloudy glass, a pallor in the dark and the moon.

He swore under his breath and opened the window so that she could slip in. She did so, peering anxiously about in the dark to be sure they were alone; and then with relief she patted him on the arms, chattering at him. He kept the gun to his side, out of sight, glanced anxiously at the open window, that let in a chill wind.

"Ssam," she said.

"Happy to see me, are you?" He took her by the arm to draw her out of the open. "You stay—stay there, Sazhje."

He wrapped a robe about himself and pocketed the gun, tied the sash, then looked at Sazhje, who, ignoring his advice, had perched on the foot of the bed in the moonlight. Outside, the uproar had reached the yard, angry men looking for the intruders.

"You hear that, Sazhje?" He gestured toward the window. "They're looking for *you*, Sazhje."

Curiously, she seemed to understand some of that. She glanced toward the window and then laid a long-fingered hand on her breast. "Sazhje ahhrht. Ahhrht."

"I'm glad you think you're all right. They'll shoot you, don't you understand that? Why did you come back?"

She frowned and wrinkled her flat nose. "Ah?" she asked, and then as if she determined that whatever he could answer was of no importance, she went to the window and looked out.

"No," he said sharply, and took her back from the window. The move frightened her. Her ears went back and her eyes went wide, but not in the attack pattern. It was simple alarm.

Steps ascended the stairs like thunder, and before there was time to think what to do, someone was pounding at the door.

"*Merritt!*" Porter shouted, and flung open the door without any further warning.

With a shriek of alarm Sazhje compressed her fluid body and fairly flew out the open window, while Merritt stepped into Porter's line of fire. Porter came forward as if he had thought it accident, intent on firing after the intruder; and his florid face took on outrage when Merritt barred his way.

"You *invited* that in?" he asked, incredulous. Merritt was aware of the others crowding the room, the balcony outside—of Meg, of Andrews, of a dozen others.

"It was Sazhje," he said. "I don't think she meant any harm."

"Listen," said Porter. "I ran up here thinking they'd forced an entry; we saw the window open from out back. I couldn't think anyone could be that thick-witted. What if others had followed her? What if they'd gotten into the house? We could have all had our throats cut. And who's to know she isn't one that was with them when the warehouse burned?"

"She wasn't."

"Are you in a position to know that?"

Merritt had felt that one close about him even before his own denial was out of his mouth. He glanced at Meg: she said nothing. Somewhere outside there was the report of a rifle.

Merritt turned to the window and looked out. He could see nothing.

"Worried for her?" asked Porter. "You might have shown a little of that same concern for us, in what you did."

Merritt looked about again. "I won't argue with you," he said. It seemed scarcely the moment for it. Even Andrews looked disgusted with him, but had the loyalty to move people out, to start sending them back to their rooms. Porter walked out; and finally there was only Meg left.

"Aren't you going to close the window?" she asked him in a thin, hard voice.

He turned and did so, and she was still standing there when he turned again.

"She came to the window," he said. "I knew who it was. I let her in because I was afraid someone would shoot her."

"If I see her again," said Meg. "*I'll* shoot her."

Her attitude caught him entirely off-balance. "I knew you'd be upset," he said, "but if that's the way you feel, you had your chance to say something to Porter, about Sazhje coming before."

"I'm not aiming at you. But, Sam, you'd better

remember this: if you can't bring yourself to get rid of that thing you brought us—"

"There's no harm in her."

"Then believe what you want to believe, but I'm beginning to understand that you were right how different we two are. If you can't straighten out in your mind which species you prefer, *I* can. I suppose it means very little to you, but I've been stung before where you're concerned, and I think this time I'm cured. My father's dead, thanks to them; and for all I know, it was your Sazhje that led them over the wall. And if you have no more respect for our feelings or even our safety than to do something like this—I hope they got her, Sam. I hope they did."

"You can believe this: I won't stop till I find out."

"How often have you seen her, Sam?"

"I don't see how that matters. Or what are you after?"

"If I knew what *you* were after, I'd be satisfied. Why do you even care about that thing? Why is it so important in the face of everything else that's happened? Why can't you *kill* it?"

"Is that really what you want?"

"Is it so impossible?"

"She can feel, Meg."

"Do you care so much that I can?" she returned, and slammed the door as she left.

It was chill in the forest, at this hour when the sun was just rising, before many people back at the house were even out of bed. Merritt trod carefully on damp leaves, aware how great a sound even that made in this stillness, a quiet not even the wind disturbed.

He had hoped that Sazhje would somehow be waiting for him where she had before, and that he would not have to draw the whole forest's attention to himself. But she was not, and he forced the sound from himself and called her name aloud.

The only thing it raised was a little scurrying in the leaves, something too small to see as it bounded away into the brush.

"Sazhje!" he called again.

He left the trail in the direction that she had tried to draw him that night of the fire, and called her name again and again, until he thought there must be nothing in the forest that was unaware of his presence.

Something rather larger was coming his way; and he drew his pistol and waited as the rustling of leaves and brush came closer to him.

"Sazhje?" he asked of the presence beyond the trees.

She was there, closer than he had thought. She came round the trunk of a tree and stopped there, holding to it nervously.

"Ahhrht?" she asked him. "Sazhje ahhrht?"

"Sazhje's all right. Come on."

She was hurt. He saw that when she came clear of the brush. A shallow wound lay across her thigh, not serious, but surely painful. Still there was no hostility in her manner. He put the gun away and she came to him and took his outstretched hands, letting him take her over to a place that they could sit down, on an old log.

He had thought to examine the injury to see what he could do for her, but when he tried to see it she flicked her ears back and hit at him, not to hurt, not even touching him.

"No, Ssam."

"Sazhje's all right?"

"Ah," she confirmed, and put her hand on his shoulder, smiled with fanged happiness. "Ssam— come Sazhje."

"You've got a good memory, haven't you?" He was amazed that she had retained the words they had so laboriously taught her. But then she was reaching at the lunch sack he had with him, interested in that, he suspected, as much as in his presence. Likely she had not been up to hunting, or whatever it was she did to support herself. He wondered where the others of her kind were, if they would help her, of if her affinity for humans had somehow made her an outcast.

"What does Sazhje want?"

"Ap-ph," she said, and tugged pleadingly at the sack.

He unwrapped everything and gave it to her; he had thought first of her passion for apples and had brought one. Sazhje bit into it with an expression of ecstasy, but before it had all disappeared she remembered her social graces and held out the remainder to him.

"Sazhje's apple," he said. She smiled at him and finished it with two bites.

Before she was done, she had picked the meat out of the sandwiches, eaten a cold potato with a great deal of grimacing and distaste, and sampled the bread. That she rejected.

"Thanks," he said gravely, and put the bread back

into the sack for his own meal. Sazhje stretched, leaning against him in feline contentment.

"Ahhrht," she pronounced.

"I've got to go, now, you know. If I'm not at work ahead of the rest of them, they're going to be sure where I was, at least what I was up to. So—" He put himself on his feet, but Sazhje anticipated him with a twist of her body that put her in his way; her long arms extended to him, her ears back and her eyes wistful.

"No, Ssam."

"Hey," he said gently, and set his hands at her steely waist: impossible to forget that she was not of his kind, with the feel of hard muscle under his fingers, the invisible down that coated her golden skin. The face, strange as it was, had a kind of beauty about it, had its own expressions: one read emotion in the set of the brow, the tautness of the mouth, the turning of the ears—they had the smallest feather of fur at the tips, visible when the light caught it from behind—most of all in the wonderful eyes, gold-flecked brown, that could go from wide-pupilled black to limpid warmth, all iris. The long arms wrapped themselves about his neck, her face close to his, all happy, and she turned her head and rubbed her cheeks against his.

"Ssam," she contentedly.

"Listen, Sazhje." He patted her shoulder and she tilted her face up to look at him. "Sazhje—no go Ssam, understand? No go."

"Ssam come Sazhje?"

"Yes," he promised. The worry on her face changed to a grin—she was at her most alien when she smiled.

Long-fingered hands slid down his arms and let him go.

"Ssam come," she repeated as he was leaving.

"Sam's coming back," he affirmed, and turned toward the canyon.

10

Celestine bumped into the dock, and Jim Selby hurled out one of the cables: Merritt was among those who caught it . . . most of the station was down at the dock and had been since the first blast of her whistle from around the bend.

The stern cable was secured, the gangplank run out, and the cargo began to be unloaded, to be carried up the winding steps to the security of the house, bushels of vegetables and sacks of grain, food to hold the work crews for several weeks more.

"Sam," Amos Selby greeted Merritt, took his offered hand as he came ashore. "Good to see you up and walking. How are things?"

"Busy. Very busy. Come on, let someone else see to the unloading. We've had most of the crew idle today anyway."

"No trouble, I hope."

"No, just preparing for some more blasting. We'll be hard at it as soon as the dust settles tomorrow."

Jim joined them; Merritt seized his hand and grinned at him, and Jim fell in behind them on the long climb, walked beside as they passed the gates into the yard. Meg and Hannah Burns were at the door of the house, and there was a great scurrying about inside when they entered, tables being readied and a meal arranged for them.

"Sit down, sit down," Hannah urged them. "Meg, get their coats, will you?"

The coats went to their places on the pegs by the door, tea was served, and Merritt and the Selbys settled down at the table by the fire. The rivermen looked exhausted, but nothing affected their appetite for the usual meal of stew and potatoes. One bowlful and then another disappeared.

"It's a sin," said Amos Selby, "when we got people doing without downriver to keep us supplied."

"It isn't that bad, I hope," said Merritt.

"No," Jim said. "We got some families settled together in the lowlands to raise some winter crops on wild land. It's warm enough there by New Hope to get a little food even in winter. They're farming in common, just like we work the dam, men standing guard on fields round the clock. They've seen the People skulking about, but so far no one's been caught by them."

"It's a good change," said Amos. "Long time since I seen those downriver men do anything but cuss the weather and the woods and the things that run it. People got the smell of better times. They're willing to go short a little now. They got hope it's some use to have kids and clear land. It's been some years since there was much joy to get married at all on Hestia, like it was wishing something terrible off on kids just to bring them into this world. It's been years since I saw a couple able to look on kids as a blessing. But we got caught in a regular old-fashioned wedding down at Williams' place."

"Who?" asked Meg, who was refilling the tea mugs.

"Lew Williams and Liz Brown."

"She's the Browns' eldest, isn't she?"

"Second eldest. Ruth's still single.—Hey, Meg, any chance in sight here at the station?"

"I doubt it," said Meg in a chill tone, and walked back to the fire. Amos looked at Merritt with a rather taken-aback expression, and made a silent whistle against his teeth.

"Sorry," Amos said.

Merritt shook his head slowly, stared into the tea mug, turned it slightly so that the reflection broke up. "No matter," he said.

"Tell them the rest," said a voice nearby, and Merritt turned at his place to look at Ken Porter, who was offshift and sharing the next table with several other boys.

"Tell them where you spend your evenings," said the Porter boy. "And what with."

Merritt looked at him steadily, the rage knotted in his throat, robbing him of breath. Ken Porter was all of nineteen. He could stand up; he could beat the boy senseless or threaten to. There would still be the rest of Hestia. He did not move. Neither did young Porter. The boy smiled at him with the arrogance of youth.

"I don't think," said Amos, "that I'm much interested to hear."

"You're bound to," said the boy. "Tell them, Mr Merritt, where you go and what you do—tell them what you do when you're not telling us what to do."

Merritt came over to his bench and stared down at

the youth, though Jim moved to stop him from any violence.

"I've told Tom Porter and I'm telling you: if you think you have any worthwhile ideas, get out there and use them. Or do I ever see you at anything on the job, but giving others trouble or standing off to one side hoping someone else will do your work. What *are* you good for, boy?"

Ken Porter came to his feet with an obscenity half-uttered, crashed back again under Merritt's backhand, spitting blood. The table cleared, the other youths going over benches to get out of the way. The Porter boy edged back too, and Amos Selby tried to push Merritt back to the table.

Merritt gave back, turned, stopped again with his eyes fixed on Meg, who was over by the fire. She had stopped with the big spoon for the stew in her hand, a bowl that she had filled; and she had not moved. Of a sudden she threw the spoon back into the kettle and walked forward, slammed the bowl down on the table in his place so that a great brown puddle of it spilled.

Merritt met that look she gave him only for a moment and then in spite of the Selbys or the others, he walked for the door, snatched his coat off the peg and left.

It was the latter edge of twilight in the forest, only enough light to see by in that place where Sazhje was usually waiting. Merritt walked it with looks to this side and that. From moment to moment on the way he had almost turned back, thinking of the danger here: of meeting others of Sazhje's kind, less kindly.

He had come away with only the coat, no weapon, nothing.

"Sazhje?" he called, and again: "Sazhje?"

It took a while; it usually did. And then with a whisper of moving like wind through the bare branches, Sazhje was there. She stood still a moment, her eyes dilated, dark as the coming night, ears laid back. Then the ears flicked up to listen in his direction, and he knew she was reassured and would talk.

"Ssam? Ssam ahhrht?"

"Yes."

"Ap-ph?"

He instinctively felt of his pockets to see if he had anything to offer her. "No. Sam's sorry, Sazhje. No apple, no food."

He had expected her to be annoyed. She accepted the fact with a near approximation of a shrug, chirred softly and came to him. He sat down with her on a log they had used before.

"Come Sazhje," she said. "Sam ahhrht?"

She was disturbed by the strangeness of the hour; it was beyond his power to explain it, and she simply caught his mood and leaned against his arm and patted his hand with what gentle comfort she could offer.

At last an idea seemed to come to her and she looked up at him. "Ssam—want? Food?"

"No." he said. "Sam doesn't want." He sat for a long while with his elbows on his knees and stared at the leaf-blanketed ground. "Talk, will you?"

"Sazhje talk. Want?"

"Sam doesn't know what he wants."

She looked up into his face. The moon had risen,

and the clear down on her ears and body and head had silvered where the light touched it, bright as the moon itself. A long-fingered hand sought his and curled around his wrist.

"Ssam come?" she asked him, and drew him to his feet.

He had known she must have a place of her own not far from here. He had never found it, nor expected that she would show him that measure of trust. When he saw it, he knew that he would never have found it by searching.

There was a kind of burrow in the side of the ravine, deep within brush and between two large trees, partially roofed by their intertwined roots, a dark place, and ominous to a human. When she urged him to follow her farther he hesitated, but there seemed no harm intended, and the night was cold.

It was a clean place inside, larger than he had expected, lined with smooth dry leaves and pungent bits of evergreen, and with comfortably rounded sides . . . large enough even for a human to stretch out full length.

Sazhje stirred about, adjusting the burrow to her liking, smoothing leaves about. From some recess she produced a tidbit of smoked meat and offered it to him.

He refused it, from consideration of her want as much as from his own fastidiousness. She put it back in safe-keeping and then settled down again next to him.

It was warm next her body heat, and sheltered as they were from the wind. After a time he stirred himself to take off his coat and to loosen his clothing, then settled down again in comfort. Sezhje nestled against him as close as she could, and he smoothed her downy back in a way that he knew made her happy.

Her arms went about him, and mischievously she teased the hair on the back of his neck, which she knew irritated him. He reached back and slapped at her fingers and she gave a chirr of laughter and did it again. This time he reached for her hand and held it, but after a moment she was bothering him again, ruffling the hairs at his chest. He slapped at her and she laughed again and bit him where his neck met the shoulder, enough to draw an exclamation of annoyance from him. He seized both her wrists, a little alarmed.

She let herself be wrestled down easily this time, and laughed, and he stared down at her face in the moonlight that reached them through the entrance— realizing with sick shock that it was not a game she was playing.

"Sazhje," he said miserably, "you little idiot—"

She talked to him in her own tongue, linked her spidery arms about his neck and pulled her face up next to his. Merritt held her gently, and smoothed her hair and tried to talk to her. She burrowed her face under his chin and made small senseless noises at him—her sharp little teeth fastened in without hurting, though he could not but think what they could do.

"Sazhje," he said. "Sazhje, don't you know you're not the same as I am? Sazhje, stop it, Sazhje—no."

He jerked at her roughly; and she looked at him wide-eyed, ears back, lips parted so that he could dimly see those other than human teeth. For a moment he had to remember how deadly dangerous she could be when crossed, how quick and strong; and he knew her mood was not a reasoning one now. The ears stayed down, but he knew the eyes, so wistfully sad.

"Ssam," she said, and reached a long-fingered hand to his face. Her touch was very light, her peculiarly smooth fingers a strange sensation. "Ssam come Sazhje. No talk, Ssam, no, no talk. Good Ssam."

He had to smile. She threw back at him what he would say to her when she behaved. And Sazhje saw the smile and laughed and ducked her head against him, lifting it again to see his reaction.

"Sazhje," he said with a shake of his head, "there's a mind in that head of yours. There is. I wish I could reach it. I wish you could understand—so many things; and that I could understand you."

"What? What, Ssam?"

"I wish I knew myself . . . but you're not the halfwit they think you are, are you, girl? You think. You feel. And I don't know if that makes you human or not—or what it makes me."

Something stirred in the leaves outside, a curious rhythmic sound. Merritt opened his eyes on murky daylight, on leaves outside that were being spotted with moisture. It was raining.

He dragged himself up on one arm, startling Sazhje, who wakened and leaned over him to see what was the cause of the commotion outside. When Merritt edged out of the hole into the rain she scolded him as if she had lost respect for his good sense, but as he had dragged his coat out with him and she realized he was leaving, she came out too and held to his hands, talking at him and chattering with distress.

He answered her with a pat on her face, the only way he could make her know she was not to blame—and ran, ran all out, tugging his coat on whenever he must stop for breath, through a graying sheet of rain.

He reached the lookout by the dam to find the men there already: it was long after daybreak. They stood about in small groups, as drenched as he, the rain turning the gravelly earth glistening wet. Lightning lit the landscape, tinging things with white. A moment later thunder rolled from one end of the valley to the other.

Young Miller was the first to see him; and Tom Porter was the second. Merritt stopped short of the group, dead still as he saw Porter come toward him and the others group behind.

"Glad you found it important enough to be here," said Porter.

Merritt had no answer for him, felt the aura of menace as the others spaced themselves out close to him.

"Half-human," one of them said with loathing, "what's it like with her, Merritt? What's the attraction?"

Merritt looked toward the speaker. Someone else seized his arm from the other side. He spun about on reflex. It was Jim Selby.

"Bill," Jim said, "Sam's not the problem. And he doesn't question our ways, what we do. He's sweated plenty over this dam of ours. It's his plans, his work

144

before most of you even got up here. He came all the way seven years' voyage to this world of ours, and there ain't a hard job or a long one he ain't showed you how to do first. So if you got some temper to work off, you go cuss at the weather. You'll get about as much done either way."

"You choose your friends, Selby—or whatever your name ought to be. You're only a shade more Hestian than he is; and from what I've heard, his habits must run in the blood."

Merritt looked at Porter. "Is this solving anything? So you've all unloaded what you think: we haven't that much time to waste. It's your farms in the way downriver, nothing of mine."

"Oh, you have an interest in seeing that dam finished, Merritt. You got a great deal of interest— because you'll never make that starship if this project fails. You'll be with us, whatever happens."

He moved the others off with that last remark, and Merritt stared at their rain-hazed backs with a great shiver of anger, hardly felt Jim's hand on his shoulder.

"Sam. Sam, you were right. You can't fight them and come out of it alive. You had to take it, same as me."

Merritt looked at him and managed to nod agreement.

"Was it," Jim ventured, "was it what they said it was, Sam? What happened last night?"

"Is that really the issue? Does it matter to you, one way or the other?"

"No," Jim said, without needing to think about it. "But to them it does."

11

There was a wind up, in addition to the rain, a southerly wind that breathed of spring and set the rope bridge swaying. Merritt staggered on the planking and kept both hands on the ropes. Far under his feet the river was louder than usual, the enlarged flume thundering an increased flood down beyond the dam, while to the upriver the earthwork diversion dike had backed up increasingly deeper water, still water to all appearance, until it slipped violently down that chute and boiled among the rocks before it started its seaward course again.

Work was still proceeding on the far side of the dam. The crest of the dam, at last reared to respectable height and recognizable form, was aswarm with miniature dark figures: the rammed-earth and timber platform on which most of the work was done was nearly level with the dam surface. Patient oxcarts labored back and forth from the blast site to the platform where they discharged their cargoes, rock dumped and spread in endless repetition: blasting in the upper ridges, to oxcart, to the dam, like the action of ants worrying at a carcass, until the cliffs disappeared bit by bit and the dam grew.

There were no stops in the work now, not even by night. Armed crews by lanternlight, in all weather, plied the roads between the blasting area from which they took the stone, and carried the loads that daylight crews would move to more precise location. Half the human population of Hestia was encamped at Burns' Station now, in shacks, in tents, within the walls and in a wooden stockade where the sheep meadow had been: in potential population, Burns' Station was far larger than New Hope itself, if all three shifts had ever been in camp at once.

There was a trail that led past the guard station as one left the bridge. Merritt took it, moving quickly with the wind at his back, his clothing long-since drenched. His hair streamed blinding water into his eyes, his boots were over the ankle in most of the puddles, and for the rest, he was well-spattered with the omnipresent yellow clay. The rains had been a frequent thing these last weeks: not yet the full deluge that spring would throw down on them, for the icemelt of the high mountains had not yet joined it; but there was an endless seeping moisture driven on the winds, dripping from ropes and hair and making the clay and rocks of the upper slopes treacherously slick.

Andrews was standing where the road from the blast site and that from the dam met the trail from the bridge. Merritt came up behind him and stood beside him as they waited for one of the lumbering, perilously loaded oxcarts to make its way past and enter the tortuous downward road to the plateau by the dam. Joints groaned, wooden wheels scraped and bumped over the rock, and the patient animals made the first turn. A hand-sized rock came loose and bounced and rattled down the road ahead of the wagon.

"We got one stuck up there an hour ago," said Andrews, who was plastered with mud more than the average on such a day. "Finally got it free, but it snapped an axle."

Merritt looked down the perilous incline the oxcart was following. It made another turn, brakes squealing, swaying the load against the wooden slats. Inexorably the whole overloaded wagon began to slew round to the curve, oxen straining in vain to hold it.

At the very last moment it stopped, with one wheel dropped over, the shaken driver screaming at the oxen and trying to make them move.

Merritt had begun to run without realizing it, Andrews hard behind him, and every other man who had seen the accident came converging on the spot. The imprudent driver, one of the Harpers, was flailing hysterically at the animals and trying to force them to move the wagon. The beasts rolled their great eyes and heaved against the weight, but it was beyond their strength to do more than maintain the pull. The effort only eroded the rain-slick clay the more and sent a miniature mudslide cascading downslope.

"Get off!" someone advised the driver. But as he tried it, the shift of weight caused the wagon to rock back alarmingly. Men cried out and braced the reachable wheels, ignoring the danger of a crumbling edge and a dizzying drop below, helped the frightened oxen bring it back into balance again.

Merritt looked at the whole thing helplessly, ignorant of the limits of the animals; but that the oxen would tire or that the rain-soft bank would give was inevitable. To unload the cart, it would be necessary to climb atop it. It would never bear the weight.

"If we pull it from the front," he suggested. "If we could get another pair of oxen . . . Has somebody got a line?"

Andrews evidently thought the plan possible. He turned off upslope at a dead run while Merritt sent another man after line and cable.

"Take it easy," he called up to Harper then. "We're going to rig a way to get you off. Don't jump unless you have to. Harris, you go down to the next turn and warn the men to clear out below. If this load gets dumped . . ."

There was no need to finish that sentence. Poor Harper sat his place very still, while men tried as best they could to help the oxen hold, to calm them and to keep them steady.

The man came back with the rope, running; but when he came close to the already nervous team, he slowed to a careful walk.

"Here," said the man. "George has them loosing a team up there. It's going to take just another minute to get them down here."

Merritt nodded, paid out sufficient line and tossed an end to Harper. "Make a safety line of that; tie it hard, so if it goes, we'll still have you with us. Just make sure you don't get tangled with it. Go off this side if you have to jump. And you tell me: do you want to jump now and lose the team and wagon, or do you want to try to get it up?"

Harper considered it, the meanwhile tying the line about himself. "I'll sit it out so far as I can," he said.

They moved in carefully with the cable, steadied the oxen while they tied the heavier rope to the wagon tree and tried to relieve the pull on the animals somewhat by their own pulling. There was some discussion of cutting harness and rescuing Harper and the animals and letting the wagon go, but the tension on the harness was too much. If the animals came free unequally, the results could be disaster for anyone involved.

With a rattling of harness and the calls of another driver, Andrews returned with his reinforcements. Harper's team shied off alarmingly, causing a new mudslide, and steadied again under the hands of the men with them.

It needed time to move the additional oxen in and to attach the harness, but then with that awesome second weight of muscle heaving in unison with the first, the imperilled wagon began slowly to move, the dropped wheel rising to find purchase against the crumbling bank.

Something snapped, a great crack of wood; and with a rumbling slide the load spilled and the main part of the wagon tilted back, while the broken tree at first let the oxen stumble forward. The wagon was over the edge, the hysterical animals being dragged backward, Harper completely out of sight though the rope in the hands of his safety men was still taut. There on the edge the wreckage hung, downed animals struggling to rise, the wagon now empty dangling in space by part of the harness and the broken understructure.

The driver who owned the second team was first to react, trying to cut both teams free; and Merritt was on the line with Andrews and the Miller boys trying to pull Harper up.

The oxen went partially free and started to their feet, lurching forward in bovine panic, and the earthen bank that had been weakened, gave. The driver and the man nearest went over, past Harper's helpless stare. The men vanished into the mud and rock downslope while above, the freed animals lunged away from restraint and shied off, wandering loose down the road at their own volition.

"Take the road down," Merritt shouted at Andrews, who was behind him on Harper's safety line. "Find those men!"

Andrews was off, providing direction for the others that were after their own fashion decided on the same. Merritt and the Millers brought Harper up over the edge safely enough, though he had not come through the ruin unscathed: his right arm hung useless, his face gone ashen.

"Take care of him," Merritt told the Millers, and stumbled to his feet. He headed down the winding road toward the base of the slide, passing the confused oxen, who were still ambling along at their own pace.

There were three litters that they took back across the swaying bridge and through the forest road to the station: one alive . . . Harper, with his broken arm; and two dead . . . the driver Wylie, and a Burns cousin, Ron Ormstead, corpses coated in yellow mire and decently wrapped in workmen's coats.

The pale-shaded mud colored the would-be rescuers too, tired men with eyes bloodshot and alive in faces that looked no different from those of the corpses. It set them apart from those that lined the approach to the main house, who stood quietly, rumor running softly through the crowd about them, who it was and what had happened.

When the silence was broken, it was by the kinsmen who came pushing their way forward to take the litters from fatigue-numbed bearers, to go with them into the bath-shed: it was where they always went from work to wash the mud off themselves, when working clothes had to be stripped off and the mud washed out of them in yellow streams of liquid clay. Now there was nowhere else to clean the dead for decent burial, or to take the filth of those who had recovered the bodies.

It was a grisly job, but on Hestia there were no professionals, no medics to take charge. Male relatives and those who had been present at the accident washed the dead, wrapped them in clean sheets for burial, cleaned up Harper and set and splinted the broken arm, all without benefit of anesthetic: the only surgeon on Hestia was apprentice-taught and resident downriver.

And afterward was the matter of bathing and changing clothes, all in the same wooden building.

Some of the boys retrieved clean clothing for them from the house and their quarters, wherever they happened to be; and by the time they had bathed and changed it was almost four hours since the time of the accident, and the sun was inclining toward the horizon.

Merritt limped out with the rest of them, holding his sodden boots in one hand, walking the trail of split logs to the front door of the house.

He did not notice Tom Porter standing on the porch until he was almost on him, or he would have avoided the confrontation; he would have backed away from it if his mind could have reached for some means to do so, but he plodded on, not looking at the man, trying not to look at him.

"Merritt. What happened out there?"

"Let be," Merritt said quietly. Porter moved into his path. He stopped.

"What happened?"

"There was an accident," Merritt said with a great effort at self-control. "There was a slide."

"I know that. But who was in charge over there?"

"Andrews and I." Merritt drew a deep breath and let it go, making up his mind to talk. "The cart was overloaded for conditions as they were. It couldn't take the first stage down. We'd have saved Harper anyway; it was trying to cut the animals free too that lost the lives. We've got four live oxen, two men dead. We're going to have to cut some timber and shore up that road: there was a considerable undercut."

"If we lose another wagon, we'll be making that trip with handbarrows."

"I know it."

"Who's working out there? It looked like the whole shift came back."

"It did. We're changing early."

"The men here in camp haven't been on off-shift. They've been cutting timber. You've got no call to take that on yourself."

153

"Take a look at the men who came back with me. We've excavated half a hillside recovering Wylie and Ormstead, and no stops for rest. They'll go back a little early each watch; but you send the others out."

Porter shook his head. "No, Mr Merritt, you go explain it to them. That can be your job; you bargained for it. I'm tired of your handing the dirty work to me."

Merritt glared at him, understanding all too well how Porter wanted the less popular orders all to come from Sam Merritt; and Porter knew that he knew, which made the moment all the more pleasurable to the man, brought the glint of self-satisfaction to Porter's little eyes. Merritt wanted to hit him; but he was civilized and ship-trained, and did not react to first impulses. He was tired, and could not think of anything to do or say. He only stood there as Porter came off the step and rudely brushed against him: the big man nearly put him off the walk into the mud.

Merritt drove all the force of his arm behind the blow, an instant ahead of the clear realization that he was going to regret doing it. The sight of Tom Porter skidding off into the mud to land on his side like a beached fish was not an amusing one, although it ought to have been. There was no amusement either in the eyes of the men, only discomfort to have witnessed this between the men who directed them, and at such a time. As for Porter, he picked himself up—covered with yellow mud on one side—and stood there with damaged dignity staring at Merritt, making the next move his.

There was nothing to say to the men, nothing to

Porter, except that there was work that wanted doing. Merritt found the unpleasant announcement his after all. It was all that would send the witnesses on their way.

But against those adamant faces it was impossible to do anything or to say anything. If he gave an order sending a shift back to work likely they would not move, and it would be Porter who would send them on their way. With feelings high and dead awaiting burial, it was not the moment to force anyone. Better the site stay idle till the third shift's legitimate turn at least, rather than bring things to open mutiny, with Porter the offended party.

Merritt turned abruptly and took the steps to the porch, intending to quit the field as gracefully as he could under the circumstances. But there was Meg in the doorway, so that she must move or he could not pass. He paused half a step and gave her a miserable look, then came ahead and tried to edge past.

Her hand found his arm and she went inside with him, when he had expected her to make a scene and enjoy it; and that so unsettled his reckonings that he made no objection when she guided him over to the fireside, although he had intended to go upstairs and not come down till morning. He sat down on the chair by the fire, set his boots to dry while he warmed his bare feet on the hearthstones and held his hands toward the fire.

"Want a cup of tea?" she asked him, which was the due of any man coming off work at the site. He nodded.

"If it comes without questions."

"All right." She went to the worktable beside the

fireplace, measured out the tea, poured hot water from the kettle that was always ready on its hook. She made it the way he had learned to like it, lacing it with a little of the herbal stimulant that was one of Hestia's homespun vices, a genteel wickedness.

"Thanks," he said, taking it from her hands. He drew the first sip of it, inhaling the scented warmth. She pulled a stool over by the hearth and sat down, silent.

"There wasn't anything I could do," he said finally. "Maybe if I'd stopped the man when I saw the wagon overloaded, if I'd insisted on shoring up that road earlier—"

"You can't see to everything at once."

"I saw that on its way to happen. The next moment it was too late."

"Sam," she said, and then shook her head as if she had changed her mind about what she was going to say. "Sam, you drink your tea and go upstairs and rest. I'll bring supper up to you."

"Sure," he said, and stared into the fire, unmoving. "Let me be, Meg. That's all I want at the moment."

"No one blames you."

"Don't they." He looked around at her after he had spoken the sarcasm and decided she had not, after all, been accusing him. "Haven't you been burned often enough where I'm concerned, without coming to offer me condolences now? I think they're misplaced. Ron Ormstead was your cousin."

"You always blame yourself worst over things you can't help, and never admit you're at fault for the things you really do wrong."

"Meg, let's not open that old quarrel."

"No, I didn't intend that. I didn't intend that at all."

"Enough's been said that we didn't mean, at one time or another." He drank half the cup and then the rest. "I'm sorry, Meg. I know you men well. It's appreciated."

She took the cup he handed her, and her eyes shimmered with tears, her hair red-dyed with firelight. There was a fragile tenor to the moment, such that he stopped with his hand not quite back to himself, and drew back more slowly.

"The trouble is," she said, "that we always meant what we said. You told me a long time back that I was only backriver Hestian, and awfully naïve. You were right, of course. You could have talked me into anything then, if you'd only been able to lie a litle."

"I didn't mean it against you, Meg."

"I know. I'd have made us miserable, wouldn't I, because I'd have expected you to behave in a way you just can't."

"I don't look for ways to cause trouble. They just come."

"Because you walked into a kind of war—us and this river and all that goes with it. And you don't get concerned when we do and *you* get concerned when we don't. Maybe you even figure you can afford to lose; after all, your Earth goes on somewhere even if you get killed out here. But ours doesn't. It dies here, all in this one valley, for good and forever, Sam. And that doesn't seem to frighten you. You keep talking about the future, and we just want to live through this one year. Maybe someday we'll have the heart to worry over the things that worry you, if we live. But sometimes we get the impression you won't be entirely sorry if that dam doesn't get built."

"Not true." It hit him like a blow, like Porter out front, and the anger swelled up in him. "Not true, no, it's not true."

"And what about Sazhje?"

He looked at her. It was a name she had not mentioned in a very long time. "I know that dam's got to be built this year. I'm doing it. And I also know that every load of rock we put down is one more step toward wiping out another species, one that was in this valley before humans ever set foot on Hestia. Don't you think of it? Doesn't it matter to you at all? It ought to."

"It ought to; and it doesn't. That's the sore spot, isn't it?"

"I can't understand that attitude in you. I can't understand it."

"We want to live. And there's no way her kind and ours can both survive. It's our lives, my friends' lives that matter."

"I can't accept that there are only those alternatives."

"Don't you?" Her eyes looked pained. "At times, Sam, I have this awful feeling that Hestians and Sazhje's kind are just about equal in your eyes, because neither of us is really yours. You're a good man; you mean well. But I wish I knew to which side first."

"I'm working—I've worked, day to dark, after. Or is that nothing?"

"Everyone appreciates that. But how much is it worth, Sam, when everyone knows you'd be off to the

Upriver and Sazhje if you weren't watched? And you are watched, you know. You can't have missed that."

"No, I haven't missed it. Porter's boys are easy to spot, especially when they walk me home and back."

Meg's lips tightened. "Sam, I saw—I saw what you did to Porter out there. My dad's not here any more. Things are different. Don't you know you can't win against them? You have to have the Porters' help if you're ever going to reach that starship when it comes."

"I know the score, Meg. You're telling me no news."

"Do I have to spell it out? There are some of Porter's men who'd kill you as soon as not. They're that way. And when the dam's finished and there's no more need of you, you've got to take that ship off Hestia. You've got to. You've left yourself no choice."

Merritt gave a tight smile. "That dam's past the stage that I mean anything essential to the effort. They have my notes. They won't let me touch them myself without someone of theirs to guard me. The foremen know their business by now. But Porter won't see me killed. It could be a long time before Hestians think they've exhausted all the projects Sam Merritt could design for them. And as you say, there's no law out here, nothing that says I have a right to leave this world. *Adam Jones* will carry the news of what happened to me back to Earth, some years from now. And seven years after that, Earth might send a strong protest about your methods, but there'll be no force behind it. Porter knows that. He'll keep dangling the lure of passage offworld in front of me so long as I seem to believe the lie. If I let him know I see through the farce, he'll think of other means."

"Tom Porter doesn't speak for all of us. But you have a way of pulling the props out from under anyone who tries to help you."

"Like you?"

"Like me, more than once."

"I'm sorry for anything I've done that's ever hurt you; but I can't say I'm sorry for anything else."

She stared at him thinking her own thoughts for a moment, at last gave a brief sigh. "And I understand that."

"The worst of what they say of me is true. Do you understand that?"

A tiny hurt came to her eyes. "Well," she said, "I'd hoped for a little better, but I suppose I really expected it."

"You tell me this: would you take the next ship out if I could make it, now that you really know me?"

Meg smiled sadly. "Truth is, I still might. There's not a person knows me that would understand, but maybe Jim. I'm ashamed to admit it's still true."

"I wouldn't let you do it, anyway. Look at me, on Hestia. That's an example of what it is to be where you don't belong. Besides—there'll be no ships for me. None at all." He pulled on his boots and rose, paused to look back at her. "Meg," he said in leaving, "thanks for trying."

"Where are you going?"

"Out," he said, and amended: "Down to *Celestine*. I guess Jim and Amos will be there."

"Sam—"

"Don't worry about me. Your dam will get finished, one way or the other."

"That's not all that matters to me."

He considered that a moment, nodded, then turned and left.

12

"I heard rumors," Jim said. "I'm glad you got yourself
down here, Sam."

Merritt wiped his streaming hair back from his
eyes and settled against the sill inside the shelter of
the wheelhouse. They were alone, isolated by the
water that sheeted down off the roof and drowned
sounds from outside. The river pitched under them, a
steady and rhythmic bobbing under the power of the
current.

"What rumors?" Merritt asked.

"How you and Porter went at each other. How
there's some of his men talking about paying you off
for that. Sam, Sam, why'd you go and do that? You
don't cross men like Porter and go free of it. He's got
family; he's got more than—"

"Where's your father?"

"Up to the stockade. He's been there all afternoon
on something or another. Why? What do you want?"

"A small favor. Or a large one, depending on how
things work out. I want you to cover for me tonight."

"Sam—you don't mean to try to leave out of here.
No. I won't do that. Look"—he set his hand on
Merritt's shoulder. "Look, they'll calm down if you

give things a chance. You stay out of sight down here tonight, and they'll have changed their minds by morning. But you try to do something wild, like leave the station—"

Merritt shook his head slowly. "I'm going, Jim."

"There's no way back if you do."

"Yes, there is, even if they learn I'm gone. What can they do about it? Put me under guard? They've done that. Or worse? Not while they think they can have my help for other projects. But if I don't go now, if I don't take this chance, I may not find another— not in time for Sazhje. I can talk to her a little; I can warn her, I think. I intend to try. Maybe they have sense enough to know what's coming. I don't know. But I want to help her if I can."

"And if they learn what you're up to they'll kill you."

"I doubt it very much at this stage. Jim, I can make it if you'll cover for me. I've got it figured, in this rain, with them knowing I'm down here—all I have to do is walk back to the dock, round that bend and into the trees again, and all it takes is for you not to give the alarm."

"And if something goes wrong, if they know—"

"I'm asking it of you because I thought you of all the others might understand why I'm doing this. But if it's too much risk, just say so, and don't admit you ever saw me today. This may be my last chance, Jim, the last ever for Sazhje's kind; Porter may not let me get loose again. But for this one time I'm going to do what I want, and you know I've thought it out already. I really figure they won't lay a hand on me;

but if I'm wrong my chances weren't much anyway, no matter how well I behaved."

"I don't think even my father's going to understand this time. Or forgive you. But that doesn't matter, does it?"

"What's your answer, Jim?"

Jim shook his blond head, looked up frowning. "If you're quick, if you're back by morning, I'll lie for you. I'll say you slept on *Celestine*, and Dad won't call me a liar or you either. Can you make it back in one night, all the way around and back?"

"What about your father? I don't want to hurt either of you. What would they do at worst?"

"Huh. They need us as much as they do you. I'll tell Dad after it's too late to stop you. He'll cuss your lack of good sense, but he's not going to give Porter what he needs to hang you. He doesn't like Porter any better than you do. Besides, if they get onto it before you get back—I'll just be working here, and I'll never notice that you didn't go back up those steps when you leave the boat." He worked out of his jacket. "Here. Take this. It's heavier than yours and drier. Besides, there's a dozen like it in camp; and you might have picked it up same way you leave the boat, while my back is turned."

The clouds were ragged and sparse and the moon was up when he approached Sazhje's burrow: the moonlight was enough to light the way through the woods. But there was already worry gnawing at him, the same that there had been from the moment he conceived the plan: that there would be no Sazhje. It had been a long time since he had last seen her; how long her memory or her patience might be he did not know. Loneliness might have drawn her back to her own kind long ago and put her out of reach.

He went quietly down the ravine. There were the well-remembered trees that tangled their roots into the hill, the dark doorway. He gave a low whistle, and called her name aloud.

There was no response.

He came closer and looked inside, and crept in and felt of the leaves that lined it, his heart sinking with the confirmation of his fears. No body warmth lingered there; there was no sign of an occupant his coming might have startled away. She was gone.

"Sazhje!" he called aloud to the listening forest, and waited. Nothing broke the silence. "Sazhje!"

At last in despair he started away, to trace his long way back to *Celestine*. Jim had risked enough for his sake, and there was nothing to justify increasing the debt. He had tried, and more than that he could not do.

A body whispered through the bare trees over his head, and he stopped, looked up, saw moonlight limning a body in silver.

"Sazhje?" he questioned, and knew his mistake as the creature moved. He knew Sazhje's delicate grace, and this body was different, more solid and angular. That realization came simultaneous with the remembrance he was not armed.

More brush stirred behind him. He spun about to meet the threat and saw another of Sazhje's kind, a tall male that went as naked as Sazhje, but for a knotted strip about his waist and a knife in his right hand. There was no question about his intentions. He sidled forward at a crouch, mobile ears laid flat against his elongate skull, eyes black and dangerous in the dim light.

The one from overhead chattered something, and the other answered and grudgingly held back. The ears did not lift; and the eyes held nothing less of that unreckoning wildness.

Brush slithered and crackled from behind and Merritt turned on one heel; the other had hit the ground. A hurtling body took him chest-high and he hurled his own weight against the attacker, trying to keep his own chin down and reach the creature's throat with his fingers. But if Sazhje had been strong, the strength of this adult male of her kind was incredible. Merritt used his weight and his height: it was the only advantage humanity gave him; and he was able to push the creature down and pin it briefly, even then wondering why the one behind him was holding off.

Then inexorably, long-fingered hands closed on his arms and pried his hands apart, breaking his grip on its throat; and with snakish agility those slim legs found leverage and the creature heaved free of him, hit him when he was trying to rise and carried him over, on the bottom of it this time.

The deadly fangs came within a little of his throat, but Merritt twisted, got his legs under him and hit with a supreme effort, too close to miss.

The blow met solid muscle, no yielding; and the creature let out a spitting snarl, launched forward with real temper this time. Powerful teeth sank into Merritt's blocking arm, ripped, and when he won free of that mauling attack and staggered for his feet, another rush carried him against a tree and almost over.

He lurched up, shouldered the creature low and hard, at once tangled in a sinuous grip and twisted onto his back, long fangs sunk into his arm.

Almost he heaved free again, but now the other entered the fight, pinning his numb and bitten arm, adding its weight to the other's. Merritt struggled wildly, his own sounds by now indistinguishable from the guttural hisses and snarls of his attackers. He tried to keep his chin down; it did not work. The creature broke his defense and clamped fanged jaws onto his throat, growling and worrying like an animal. The blood shut off, air as well, Merritt struggled the more frantically for a moment, and began to weaken, but the jaws closed no further— shook at him vengefully every time he struggled and let up the pressure when he lay still. At last when that fact had reached his numbed brain and he stopped fighting, the creature let go that hold and leaned on his arms, staring down at him.

It was a terrible sight, this male version of Sazhje's face; ears flat, nostrils distended, eyes dark and murderous—lips drawn back in a snarl that showed fangs that made Sazhje's seem ineffectual. The arms and shoulders that bore down on his arms were powerful beyond any expectation from size alone. He could gain nothing against that grip, and both hands were losing their feeling.

Carefully the creature released him and stood back, and the companion too, so that Merritt was free to gain his feet. He gathered himself and staggered, wounds beginning to throb with dull misery.

The nearer one spoke at him: he could understand nothing of it, and the one behind was clearly growing impatient, gesturing with his stone knife and urging something with short and guttural syllables. The first one silenced him with a terse spitting sound and turned back to Merritt.

"Sazhje?" the creature asked.

Merritt tried the best he knew to sign affirmative. "Sam," he said of himself, touching his chest. "Call Sazhje. Tell Sazhje."

The creature silenced him with a snarl, indicated himself and something that involved Sazhje's name, motioning for him to move.

Merritt hesitated and the other backhanded him with bonejarring force, sent him stumbling aside in the direction they wanted him to go. It was a measure of their confidence that they put no restraint on him, but pushed him from time to time where they wanted him to turn, contemptuous of his power to escape them even in the thickets and brush that were close on either hand.

They rested toward dawn somewhere so far into the deep forest that Merritt had no idea where they were. His two captors secured his hands most uncomfortably about a tree with their cord belts and curled up contentedly to sleep for a few hours, while he took what rest he could upright, with his hands numbing.

Then they were moving again, descending from the heights into a boggy area that was no doubt formed by some tributary of the river. It was hard traveling: wading part of the time, walking in mud and wet reeds the rest, and Merritt's sodden boots began to come apart and to gall his feet.

The second and the third nights were increasing torment. When they slept, which was usually by three-hour periods, Merritt spent the time wet and shivering, while the others curled up back to back on the driest spot or singly in the crotch of some tree; and Merritt began to develop a nagging cough ... beyond pain, he ceased to care about anything but opportunities to rest.

His clumsiness on the march irritated Rejkh ... Rejkh the surlier of the two. The one who had subdued him in the first place was Otrekh, a big, almost good-natured fellow of some patience; but from time to time the smaller male would exercise his temper by pushing at Merritt, and sometimes by kicking him when he was slow in rising.

And since the kick was low and foul, Merritt caught his breath finally and walked obediently enough for the better part of the morning; but ideas of escape had been replaced with a simpler, more achievable purpose. He did entirely as pleased Rejkh, ducked his head and hastened when Rejkh snarled at him, and flinched from every threat.

And then they crossed a small stream by way of a log lying across it, and Merritt looked down into the deepish waters with a certain satisfaction. Rejkh gave him the usual push in the back for the delay, and cuffed him on the side of the head.

With a snarl no more human than Rejkh's, Merritt surprised him with a waist-high rush that carried them both over, and got a choking grip on Rejkh's throat, holding him under.

Rejkh flailed and squalled, choked and choking, and suddenly more interested in escape than combat. Air bubbled up.

A blow exploded across the base of Merritt's skull and a powerful arm encircled his neck from behind, jerking him loose from Rejkh, who stumbled dripping and retching to his feet and attacked. Merritt kicked, and suddenly found himself underwater, until he sucked water and choked. Then they dragged him sodden and feebly struggling to the bank.

There Rejkh as well collapsed and began to cough up the water he had swallowed; and Otrekh began to make a strange sound that Merritt recognized as laughter, his fanged face split in a fearsome grin. He slapped Rejkh on the shoulder in high amusement at Rejkh's expense.

Rejkh grumbled something in reply and got to his feet, kicked Merritt to make him move, and Merritt added the score for himself and stumbled up to his feet. Then Rejkh dealt him a ringing slap, and he spat blood and flung himself for Rejkh's throat again, but Otrekh seized his arm and swung him aside, holding him back, still laughing softly.

"*Ssam, Ssam khue*," said Otrekh, which Merritt had learned was an order to move. Merritt shot a look under his brows at Rejkh and did so. Otrekh jerked at the arm he held and told him something in warning tones that did not need translating, but there was no more kicking.

Rejkh followed, still grumbling to himself.

For most of the rest of the day they were climbing, by narrow trails and through undergrowth, losing altitude at times as they crossed narrow stream-cut ravines, but always working higher. His boots almost gone by this time, his feet cut by stones which his barefoot captors ignored, Merritt tried toward evening to sit down and rest, which in days before even Rejkh had tolerated; but this time they put him on his feet the third time with no gentleness about it. When he gestured, asking them at least for food, they snarled at him and made him move on.

Soon he understood their lack of patience, for they were coming into an area of many trails, a blind valley with a stream trickling through it, and at its far side, near one old, old tree, burrows were made in the hillside, and others dotted a mound that might have been artificially reared. The homes, surely homes, were faced on the front with rock, with tiny windows and smallish doors which used stone or wooden lintels for support. Those on the hill had the most improbable accesses, winding trails over the porch of one to reach the door of the next, a maze of stone terraces and paths, with rocks neatly and decoratively arranged. There was a certain charm about the place until they came into the well-worn center ground of the village under that ancient tree; and Merritt saw the fruit the branches bore—bleaching skulls, not human, but of their own kind, hung up like ornaments.

Otrekh gave a shrill call and inhabitants spilled forth from burrows and from hilltops and the woods themselves, male, female, young ones that scampered about and shrieked in imitative hostilities; and old ones that walked stooped and shuffling. The young

males ventured closest, and one brandished a knife
and yelled as if working up nerve for a charge.

Merritt realized at the last instant it was no bluff;
he sprang back from the rush and escaped with a
burning scrape of the stone knife across his ribs, the
cloth parted, but his skin intact. Others hit him then,
snarling and clawing.

And Merritt dived for the one that had started the
attack, seized him, single-mindedly trying to beat the
life out of his ugly face before the others reached his
throat; but they pulled him off and threw him from
one to the other, laughing and chirring in raucous
amusement, tearing at his clothes, which seemed
particularly to attract them.

A hand seized his collar and pulled him back from
the midst of it, and Otrekh waded into the midst of
the youths with a mighty backhand that cleared them
back to a respectful distance. Merritt shook the hair
from his eyes and struggled to loose himself from the
grip that held him, finding it Rejkh; but Otrekh came
then and seized him from the other side, hastening
him along with no gentle urging.

Under the branches of that ominous tree Otrekh
finally stopped and let him go; and Rejkh released
him more rudely. A young female came running and
hugged Otrekh and then Rejkh in welcome; and then
she turned her face toward Merritt.

It was Sazhje. Among all the alien faces he knew
her. It was the look in her eyes.

"Ssam," she said then, and that was all; but there
seemed a note of pity in her voice.

Older males came, and a few old females of very
great age; and Sazhje interrupted as Otrekh began to

talk with them. When they ignored her, her voice rose shriller than theirs and more insistent, and she gestured furiously and then pleadingly until one of the elders threatened her with an uplifted hand. Otrekh put her out of the discussion with a brutal slap that made Merritt's teeth ache in sympathy.

Poor little Sazhje stumbled backward, recovered herself with a hiss and a baring of teeth, but when Otrekh growled and lunged at her she moved quickly enough out of his reach and slunk off with backward looks and growls in her throat.

Other females had gathered, and began to gather about Merritt, fingering him and his clothing in curiosity; and some of the youngest males were with them. Sazhje moved in on them to vent her fury, snarled and spat and sent them running—even Rejkh, who had the weight to win but chose to retreat. Sazhje put her arms about Merritt then and talked to him sympathetically, patted him and kept hold of his hand even while she turned and pricked up her ears to listen to the discussion Otrekh was having with the elders.

"Sam's not all right, is he?" Merritt said to her, and her long fingers tightened on his hand.

"Ahhrht," she insisted, and he had never imagined he could detect a lie in that unhuman voice. Sazhje was afraid. Her nails bit into his palm until they hurt, and she never ceased to listen to what was being said in the circle until the discussion was done.

Then as the council broke up, she dropped his hand and thrust herself forward once more, keeping out of Otrekh's reach and shouting at them, making fists of her slim hands and pounding them on her thighs to emphasize the point she was making.

At last Otrekh seemed to assent to what she was saying. He returned to Merritt along with Sazhje and seized his arm, let him up along a steep trail to a burrow about halfway up the hill. Rejkh and a few others trudged along behind.

Merritt knelt and crawled inside as they seemed to wish of him; and one of the adult males remained on guard outside, an effective prison, for there was only one exit possible and he must come out on hands and knees.

He tucked up then, and simply rested, numb to anything else.

Night came, dim and starlit, and the noises of the camp died away, but for the rustling comings and goings to burrows.

And finally a silver-outlined shadow appeared against the opening, and came inside with him.

"Ssam," said Sazhje's voice, and light fingers touched him in the darkness. He put his hand out to her arm and she leaned over and touched her lips to his face, a human gesture she had learned of him one night long past: as her face was constructed it was rather a chaste and dry expression, but one of utmost tenderness; and he wished earnestly he had words to talk with her.

She returned to the entrance and drew gourd containers in with her, food and drink, which she offered and he took gratefully, not caring what the food was.

"Thanks," he said hoarsely when he had done, and she reached up and fingered his unshaven face, then with gentle tugs at his collar urged him to put off his damp and filthy clothing.

He did so. She treated his hurts as was apparently the method of her kind, with her mouth and with water from the gourd: and she sealed the worst ones with what felt like quick-drying clay. It eased the fire in them. He did not judge his future long enough to worry for infection. The moment's comfort was enough.

When she was done she stirred the rushes that lined the burrow into a nest and settled down beside him, warming him with her body until he could relax for the first time in days. He lay with his head against her and even slept for a time, until her stirring wakened him.

"Sazhje?" he murmured, only then realizing he had slept. Her gentle fingers pushed at his shoulder and he moved, aware he had been causing her discomfort.

"Good Ssam," she murmured in his ear.

"Sazhje—Sam came, Sam came to find Sazhje."

"Ah," she acknowledged. "Ssam no come, Ssam no come, 'morrow, 'morrow, 'morrow. Sazhje go Sazhje people. Poor Ssam. Otrekh come Ssam."

"Is Otrekh Sazhje's?"

"Otrekh—" Sazhje hesitated over that a long time, trying evidently to discover words for what Otrekh was to her. He thought that it was probably kinship, since Otrekh had not objected to Sazhje's joining him in the burrow—supposing that Otrekh knew where Sazhje was at the moment.

"Sazhje," he said, "Sam came to tell Sazhje—the dam—you remember, the dam—"

"Ah." She made a pyramid of her hands: she knew

175

what it was that he built every day; he had tried to explain it to her one morning. "Tam."

"High water's coming, Sazhje. The dam will hold the water. Hold, you see. Water will come Sazhje people, Water—"

"Wa," she affirmed. She had never been able to pronounce that word.

"Water come Sazhje people. Sam came to tell Sazhje—"

"*Ah.*" Understanding dawned in her voice. "Ah. Ah, Ssam. Sazhje people—Sazhje people no ahhrht."

"Yes," Merritt said. "Sazhje tell her people to run—understand, run."

She made a sound that was her best approximation of *understand*, and he knew by the tension in her body that she was alarmed. Suddenly she edged toward the doorway.

"Ssam," she said, pausing, and seemed to be searching for words. "Good Ssam," she concluded helplessly, and was gone.

13

"Ssam khue."

Merritt rolled over as the guard shook at his ankle,
still bewildered with sleep and momentarily unable
to recall what his situation was. But Rejkh's heavy
hand had lately taught him how short their tempers
were, and that reflex had him crawling out of the
burrow before his mind was clearly working. It was a
strange male that had summoned him. He reached
into the burrow on hands and knees and pulled his
clothes out, partially dressed before the fellow lost
patience with him; he shrugged shirt and jacket on
while he walked.

From the hillside path he could look down on the
center of the village, on the top of the aged tree with
its awful ornaments. There was a gathering beneath
its branches, apparently most of the population of the
village, and he did not like the prospect of that.

When he reached the foot of the path and the
bottom of the hill he could hear somewhat of the
proceedings: it was a chant, one speaker alternating
with a rhythmic slapping of thighs and palms, the
group seated now on the ground about that tree. The
guard pushed him forward and he went perforce

toward it, more than apprehensive. There was a sudden hush, the chant broken at his approach.

Sazhje sprang up from among them and met him, seized and held his arm in a gesture of comfort; and now Otrekh rose to his feet and assisted a very old male to rise. There was a great deal of chattering of a sudden, but Rejkh shouted something and things grew quieter. Otrekh delivered a vehement address to the group and to the elder, and Merritt watched reactions anxiously; but beside him Sazhje remained unperturbed.

At last the others began to beat their hands upon their thighs and to chant one syllable over and over. It was bedlam, and Merritt would have stepped back but for Sazhje's forbidding hold on his arm.

Suddenly the commotion ceased, and the group fragmented, scattering in all directions, the young quickly and the elders in their own time, until what remained was a group of young males, all fitted with weapons; and this too Merritt regarded with mistrust, but Sazhje kept firm hold of his arm and hugged it with all her might when Otrekh spoke to her. There was a sharp exchange; she bounced one taut gesture of seeming triumph, looked up without letting go.

"Ssam come," she said. "Sazhje people come Gairh people. Ssam ahhrht. Ssam come ahhrht."

The young males were grouping for a journey, on a track back the way they had come; and he was going, and Sazhje was going with him. He understood finally, not where they were going, unless it was some other, more important camp, but that he was safe for the duration of the journey and Sazhje believed it. Rejkh was with them, and Otrekh: Rejkh would have come near him, but Sazhje hissed at him and Rejkh changed his mind at once. They started to move, making an irregular column going out of the village, with the young scampering along beside until they reached the first shadow of the trees. And Rejkh cast sullen glances, but Merritt gave him none back, reckoning that to be free to walk, with Sazhje holding his hand and walking with him was as much as he could ask and more.

"Where?" he asked Sazhje, making a snaking gesture to the winding trail before them. "Where Sam-Sazhje go?"

"Gairh people," she said again. "Tam." She turned her head to look at him as they walked, her face touched with deep concentration. "Gairh people no good, no good Ssam people."

That was ominous enough, if the words put themselves together in a straight line.

"Friends to Sazhje?" he supplied the word he thought she might want.

She frowned. No, that was not it. She took her hand from his to make a pyramid of her fingers. "Tam?"

"Yes, the dam. I understand."

The pyramid fell down. "Kill tam."

"What, kill the dam?"

"Ah. Ah. Gairh people kill tam. Kill Ssam people."

Merritt frowned, searched for words. For the next several moments, until Sazhje quite tired of the conversation, he tried to learn what she meant; but it was beyond their composite vocabulary. Even Otrekh joined them and fell into the argument; and Rejkh tried to explain by signs and symbols and angry gestures, but at last Merritt had to conclude only that people at their destination were going to kill the dam. It would come out no other way.

And when he tried to ask what would become of him, Otrekh and Rejkh drew out of the conversation.

"Kill Sam?" he asked.

"Ssam ahhrht." That was all that Sazhje could manage to tell him, and she seemed to say it with less than complete conviction.

A little before camp that evening it began to cloud over; and twilight came early, but there was no rain. They were on high ground already, having branched off the trail they had used on the way in some time earlier, and they settled down for what, among their kind, was a normal stop, short, according to human need for sleep.

Rejkh pushed Merritt over to a convenient tree, in what had become nightly ritual, intending to secure him for sleep; and Sazhje fairly exploded with outrage. She screamed and gestured wildly, disturbing the whole camp, and snarled first at Rejkh and then at Otrekh, and at others who had joined the quarrel, so that Merritt began to fear for both their lives in all the spitting and growling. The males swung at her and twice actually struck her with their open hands, to no avail. But finally Otrekh dealt her a blow clearly audible, and she staggered and whimpered and slunk aside.

"Otrekh!" Merritt shouted, and the big fellow lowered his ears and growled, still not offering to attack. It was all show: Merritt had almost learned to tell, and this was purely face-saving. Sazhje evidently thought so, for she gave a scornful snort and sidled her way back to take Merritt's arm.

Otrekh still had something to say; and he was not moving. This time there was hardness in his attitude, and stalemate was on them, apt to end in someone getting hurt. Merritt weighed the profit on either side and finally pushed Sazhje away, quietly went and sat down against the tree where Rejkh wanted him, and Rejkh saw to his securing with the cord, no less roughly than his habit. Sazhje watched in disapproval with much fretting and fuming, and when Rejkh was done and all the camp began to settle for the night, she came and settled at Merritt's side, worked her head under his chin and lay there hard-breathing and still angry.

"I'm sorry," Merritt told her, and her long hand patted his side comfortingly.

"Sazhje ahhrht," she assured him. "Sazhje ahhrht."

"We go to the dam, Sazhje?"

"Ah," she affirmed, and shivered against him. A few drops of rain were starting to fall. "Go tam, Gairh people tam. Ssam ahhrht. Ssam people no ahhrht. Kill Ssam people. Ssam ahhrht Sazhje."

"I don't understand, Sazhje."

"Gairh people no good Ssam people. Kill tam."

Merritt shook his head in frustration. Sazhje at her most communicative was the hardest to understand; and she looked up at him in mutual distress, knowing she had failed to make him understand all of what she was saying. At last she simply put her head down on his chest and patted him comfortingly.

The weather had been threatening all evening when they arrived at their destination, soft sea clouds slipping overhead carried on the west wind, gathering darker and darker, and the air tinged with warmth. They came early into this hillside camp, but most of the inhabitants had already sought shelter for the coming night.

There was here, as at the other location upriver, a group of burrows dug into the clay hillside. But this place had not the look of permanence such as Sazhje's village had had. Here were no stone-bordered paths, but oozing clay banks tracked into footpaths; no tidy stone-fronted residences, but rush-mat windbreaks thrust into the irregular fronts of the dwellings. All that remained the same was the centering of the camp around a particularly aged tree, which Merritt began to suspect had some religious symbolism: this one, too, was hung with skulls, whether collected from enemies killed or some grisly form of honor to their own dead.

The population was different too. In Sazhje's village there had been children, the look of a people at home and life proceeding normally. But here the residents that came pouring out of the hillside burrows to see their visitors were males and a few, a very few young females.

This, Merritt thought, looking uneasily at the gathering circle, was very probably the base of operations from which attacks on the station had been launched: no random raids by subhuman minds, but a planned campaign directed from an organized camp ... a camp known to villages and perhaps uniting several populations within it: a leader, an alien Caesar, and minds of common purpose.

And Sazhje had brought him into the center of this with her assurances of safety ... no, had come with him into this; his estimation of her promises was unhappily confirmed. Brave, stubborn Sazhje. She was firmly beside him now, her fingers entwined with his, and he realized that she was frightened too. He hoped that Otrekh could protect her; he assuredly could not.

An argument erupted in the center of the camp by the trunk of the aged tree: Otrekh and Rejkh and some of the others debating with some of the resident leaders in ear-piercing shrieks and violent gestures. Merritt turned his face away and ignored it. He was exhausted from the long walking and the sleepless nights and from hunger too, for they never gave him enough; and it seemed likely that the discussion and the shouting would go on for some time. It was apparently a matter of custom with them, this sort of loud encounter ... with what ultimate issue he did not at the moment wish to think. He saw a convenient place, a log that was perhaps intended for sitting, and tugged at Sazhje's hand, edged in that direction. She understood and went the few steps with him, sank down by him, holding his arm and enfolding his hand in hers, her head against his shoulder; but her ears flicked constantly intent on the debate in the center, beyond the crowd that curtained them from it. Torches were lit finally, and light shone through the massed bodies. The shouting became individual, one side and then the other, with the crowd shouting its own interruptions from time to time.

"What's Otrekh telling them, Sazhje? What's Otrekh saying?"

Sazhje either did not understand what he was asking in all the uproar or preferred not to answer.

She reached to pat his knee and kept her ears pricked toward the debate.

Then her fingers tensed, her free hand came back to him, a sign of caution. One of the larger males forced his way through the crowd and came back toward them and Merritt started to his feet.

He would have come willingly; he had no chance to. The strong hands closed on his sleeve and jerked him forward into the circle, spun him off-balance and into the very center by the tree.

Otrekh seized his arm and thrust him back protectively, snarling a warning at the others who started to close in. Merritt stood still, feet braced, believing for an instant that he and Otrekh were about to become the center of a fight, but the others dared nothing more than to sidle round them and make mock attacks.

Then one jumped him from behind, tried to take him away, and jerked the jacket half off him in the process, hampering his arms. There was an outburst of inhuman laughter at that, which encouraged his tormentor; the jacket came the rest of the way off, torn in the process, and Merritt staggered, nearly thrown to the ground.

Otrekh struck hands away and growled menacingly toward the most daring of the other group. Rejkh covered the other flank, baring his teeth and shrieking rage. A second sally brought Sazhje into it, her shrill voice audible over the deeper snarls of the males, and her impassioned threats and spitting growls cleared some of the less determined enemies out of her vicinity, even the bigger males either tolerant or somehow restrained from dealing with

her. It left a circle of angry argument about Merritt
that continued until he was nearly deaf with their
shouting and their screams, and at last came down to
a field of three: Otrekh and two ugly males who
seemed to be in authority over the other side . . . no
elders here; these were in their prime, and scarred
and powerful.

One of them chased Sazhje into retreat behind
Otrekh, and Rejkh joined her. Then the first round of
debate seemed ended. The sudden silence was as
unnerving as the commotion had been; and the larger
of the opposition looked at Merritt and gave a grin
that held nothing of kindness, rather served to show
his powerful fangs to better advantage. That one gave
an order to one of his subordinates, made a careless
gesture and waited, breathing hard from the violence
of the argument, while it was carried out.

Sazhje slipped back; Merritt felt her hand steal into
the bend of his elbow, her long fingers lace with his.
He was glad to have her by him.

"Ssam. Ssam, Gairh want kill tam."

The big fellow, Gairh, was going to kill the dam.
Merritt frowned in disbelief and looked to his left
again as the other one arrived bearing what he had
been asked to bring. There was a box of explosives
neatly tucked under one spidery arm: one of the
crates from the building site, one of their own; Merritt knew it by the lettering visible in the torchlight.

The bearer crouched and set it down in the midst
of the gathering, and the one called Gairh said
something with much vehemence and a showing of
his fangs. Then he pointed at Merritt; and Merritt
had a foreboding of it even before Sazhje translated.

"Gairh want Ssam kill tam."

"No," Merritt said, with no pause to weigh the answer. "Tell him no, Sazhje. Sam's not going to kill the dam for him."

Sazhje pulled furiously at his arm to make him look at her. "Ssam. No, no, Ssam. Gairh kill Ssam. Sazhje no say no Gairh, no, no, no good Ssam people, no good. Ssam kill Ssam people, stay Sazhje people."

"*No*," Merritt said. "Sam's not going to kill Sam's people. You tell Gairh no."

"Sazhje no say," she protested vehemently, and Gairh seized her by the arm and spoke to her loudly and long, something to which Sazhje responded only with distressed refusals.

Gairh thrust her away and glowered at Otrekh, then delivered an order to his lieutenant, who squatted down and stripped up the already-breached lid of the box.

Some of the upper layer of the explosives were capped and fused for firing, prepared and thrown carelessly back into the box so that the whole thing was susceptible to heat or shock. Merritt saw it and stared down at it in horror.

Someone—he could not believe it was one of Gairh's folk—had prepared some of the cylinders and turned the whole box into a bomb large enough to devastate the immediate area.

Gairh was screaming at him now, frothing with rage and passion—snatched up one of the cylinders in his fist and waved it in his direction, shouting something. Then with the other bony hand he pointed aloft and one of his people caught a limb of the tree, snatched down the object that he wanted and held it up by the hair.

The face of Dan Miller stared sightlessly back at Merritt, as Lady's had that night in the yard ... Miller, who often took the farside guard post because he liked the long in-house reliefs; who had become as expert with the explosives as Merritt, so that it was usually Miller who did the actual placing of the charges.

The creature shook the head and grimaced and screamed derisively; the others howled in chorused amusement. Merritt swallowed an upwelling in his throat and looked at Gairh.

The laughter suddenly died away and there was a moment of intense silence, no one moving. Gairh swelled up with a breath, looked as if he knew the intimidation had been effective.

With a wild howl Merritt hurled himself at Gairh's throat, carrying him over and hard against the mud.

Strong hands pried him loose from his snarling opponent, drew him back behind a wall of others' shoulders. Merritt swung to be free and suddenly felt a softer grip, heard Sazhje's voice, for Otrekh had moved in before him and Sazhje was holding to him, trying to talk sense to him, mingling words of her language and his. He gasped breath, forced himself to be calm, even while the closed ranks of Sazhje's people were all that was between him and the others, and that thin line was yielding. He stood quietly so that one of Sazhje's friends who held him would let go; and when the hands relaxed, he dived away and ran, away from the light.

"Ssam!" Sazhje's outraged shriek pursued him; and then her shrill voice was lost in such a massed howl of rage and anguish that he could no longer tell what was happening.

At forest edge and beyond, lost in the dark and the tangle, he paused to look back, realizing to his surprise each time that no one was following. The confusion that still came from the camp was such that it covered any noise he might make: and the name of it all might be Sazhje and Otrekh.

He hit the trail that led in the direction he thought the river lay, began to run, pacing himself to last. They could run him to earth once they caught his track; he had no doubt of it, but he had a few precious moments to open the lead he must somehow hold.

Or perhaps, the thought kept nagging at the edges of his mind, they were not following because they knew he would find no help: there was no knowing what might have happened at the station; and as for the connection between fire and explosives, the thought might not be too complex for Sazhje's kind, not at all.

If that box was set at the earthworks or the bypass flume, it would unleash that pent-up lake on the dam before it was ready; and if the dam failed, it would pour on the downriver a greater flood than Hestia had yet seen.

14

The dam was in sight, the gorge a brighter area in the dark. Merritt wiped the rain from his eyes and scanned the area for any sign of the enemy, aided by the lightning flashes that a moment from now must aid the enemy, betraying him to any observers as he crossed that open ground to the guard station.

He gasped another mouthful of air and stumbled ahead, slipping in the mud and the puddles, the ache in his side like a mortal wound. He had made it. He had managed to keep ahead of whatever pursuers might be behind him, and there was the goal in sight, the log shack that guarded the nearside of the bridge.

"Hey!" he hailed the unseen guards as he came within view of the slit windows. He was not about to become victim of a nervous sentry in this murk of night and storm. "Hey, in there—"

The lightning showed a pale face in the slit, glimmered wetly on a gun barrel.

"It's Merritt," he heard someone say; and then in the stop-action sequence of triple lightning flashes he saw the man lift the gun to aim.

The shot might have hit the area he vacated; he did not stop to see, not until he was well into the woods again. There was no motion of apology from the guard post. It had not been a mistake.

Shaken, trembling, he paused to wipe his vision clear again and to look over the trail behind him, anxious that the shot might have drawn his pursuers to his track. The lightnings showed him nothing but the dark trunks of trees and interlacing branches.

He sucked air and turned, started running again, the path for the ravine, the only way that was left. The river was up: he heard the thunder of it spilling off the flume; there was no time to chance the river-ward ledge, that way around under the promontory, not since the rains. He headed up, up the long incline out of the water-filled ravine, and out of the trees again. Thunder rolled down the canyon and the sound of the river roared up out of it, drowning all else.

The lights were lit, the great outer gate barred. Merritt reached the first corner of the stone wall and leaned there a moment, panting, fighting for breath. The lightning played strange tricks with the landscape, creating shadows between him and the wooden wall of the outer-camp stockade.

Ahead were the steps down, that led to the dock and *Celestine*. And before he could make the first stage, he must for a moment come under the guns of the guards at the mainhouse gate ... who just perhaps would have heard that shot from the dam; the wind and the rain could play tricks with sounds.

And perhaps *Celestine* was gone; or perhaps Amos and Jim had sheltered in the house this night. Perhaps it was all for nothing, such a risk.

He wiped at his eyes and went, keeping close to the

wall, trying to do something he had himself designed the guard-posts to make impossible—slipped along the wall in small quick moves from shadow to shadow while he could, then hit the open and sprinted for the steps.

A shot exploded behind him and kicked up water from a puddle ahead. He threw himself over the earthen bank, rolling, sliding in the clay until he bumped over the first tier and caught hold of the steps, bruised and stunned—clawed his way to them and gathered himself up, started down them, praying the Selbys would not be so quick on the trigger. An alarm dinned from the house upslope. But *Celestine* was there, riding at her moorings.

"Amos!" he shouted, slipped again on the wet boards, gathered himself and ran staggering down the heaving dock. "Amos! Jim!"

A lantern flared into the open on deck. Merritt waved at it violently, redoubled his effort to reach the gangplank before someone could get a clear shot at him from behind, outlined as he was against that light.

"It's Sam!" he heard Jim's voice across the gangway, and when he staggered out on that heaving board and leaped for the deck, friendly hands pulled him on board and steadied him.

He had no words. He slumped to the deck and leaned on his hands trying to catch his breath, the alarm up at the house still clanging in his ears, voices shouting somewhere. Amos and Jim were trying to pull him to his feet against his will, and he could not get enough breath to protest being set upright against the slot of the gangway.

"Sam," Amos said, holding his arm. "Sam, you hurt?"

Merritt shook his head, gasped down more air. In his hazed vision he saw lights start filing down the steps from the house toward the dock. Frantic, he looked toward the Selbys.

"I tried to warn them.—They fired . . ."

"We supposed to ask where you been?" Amos cut him off in a harsh tone. "Or do we just guess this time?"

"Amos—" He staggered for his feet, holding to the rail. "Amos, the People have blasting materials and they're probably headed for the dam right now."

Jim jerked him left and slammed him back against the wheelhouse, himself too stunned and out of breath to resist. He stared at Jim in bewilderment.

"How they got the stuff we already know," said Jim, his young face hard with anger. "We got Miller's body back two days after the stuff turned up missing out there at the site. But if they can use it, you tell me how they know, Sam. Or maybe the People turning up with explosives and Sam Merritt missing is supposed to add up different."

Merritt's eyes focused for a fraction of a second beyond Jim's shoulder, at the line of lanterns that had reached the dock; and snapped back to Jim's face.

"There's not much time," he told Jim. "You'd better stop them or you'll never hear my side of it."

Jim stared at him, anger still twisting his face, but he relented a little at the look Merritt gave him. He turned to one side, made his decision and picked up the rifle that lay against the rail. He threw the safety off and his father made a tentative move to stop him, then took the rifle from Jim's hand and faced the oncoming crowd himself.

"Hold your fire!" Amos shouted across the distance to the dock. "Don't you come any farther!"

"You all right out there, Amos?"

"We're fine. You just hold off, Porter. We got Merritt back. —You keep your distance, the lot of you, till I'm done talking."

"Ask Merritt where those explosives are."

"He says the People are going to blow the dam. —*Listen to me*, you—I don't know the whole story; I ain't had time to ask him, but you hold off out there till I make my mind up. And I mean that. You know I do."

"You were always blind to him, Selby—but take your time. If he's got an answer to this, let's hear it."

"I'll tell you the answer," Merritt shouted back and recklessly leaned against the railing to do it. "Miller's death was a surprise to me and so was it that they had the explosives. They got them without my help."

"We ain't sure," a new voice cut in, "but what you sent them after them for you."

"That's not true!" Merritt shouted back.

"You never wanted that dam to work, Merritt." That was Porter again. "You fought it all the way. I hear you was trying to get off this world when the governor's men caught you up in New Hope."

"I *built* that dam. What more do you want? And if you don't want it blown apart, get more guards up there on that site tonight."

"If the People can use explosives, who showed them how, Merritt? Answer us that one."

"*I* never showed them. But they're ready to fire. Maybe Miller did—I have no way of knowing."

"*That's a lie.*" The voice was that of one of the Miller cousins. "That's a rotten lie, Merritt, to save your own hide."

"I can't argue it with you, John. I don't know how they got them. Maybe they got them from Dan after he'd fixed them at the site; or maybe he meant to blow them in their camp—maybe he tried. But the People have brains to figure things out. They're intelligent beings, and they have the means to destroy the dam. Anything could set those charges off now. Maybe we'll be lucky and they'll blow themselves up before they get to the dam, but they know I'm loose and they'll know they haven't much time left. Get up there and warn those men on guard duty, whether you think I'm lying or not. There's too many of the People out there for a few rifles to stop."

"And maybe you want us all to go running off up there for reasons of your own."

"Porter," said Amos, "maybe you'd better listen to him."

"You believe that offworlder, Selby? Then you'll believe anything."

"I think we're all standing in a confounded unlucky place if that dam goes."

"*I* think he'd like to send us all up that trail into an ambush while he's at it—and leave the station unguarded."

"Are you going to send men up to the dam or not?"

There was a long hesitation, no one volunteering. "Sure," said Porter. "We'll check it out. But we'll

194

check out a few things with Merritt first. Put down that rifle, Amos. He isn't worth it."

"You do your talking from there, Porter. First man steps out front I'll try to scare him, but I can't see much in this rain and I don't want to shoot my neighbors. You just keep your distance. And while you're at it, send someone up to round up a relief party for the men at the dam, or are you just going to leave them up there alone?"

"What do we do now, Dad?" Jim asked quietly, when there was silence from the crowd.

"I think you and Sam better fire up that boiler. We got one other way out of here and besides, I don't trust Porter to send that relief party at all."

"Amos—" Merritt began, offering gratitude.

"Sam, I figuring you're telling the truth, or part of it. If I find out otherwise you'd better not be in my sights. Get moving. I don't know how close we can get old *Celestine* to that dam, but if it goes, I figure we'll be the first to know."

The wind was coming down out of the narrows, driving a blinding rain and spray against little *Celestine*, and she moved slowly, painfully slowly, her deck awash and her bow probing darkness and uncharted channel.

"Don't know how much farther we'll make it," Amos said. He took a fresh grip on the rain-slick wheel and let one hand go again to wipe his forearm across his eyes. Spray hit them and current and wind tried to turn them; Amos fought them even again, but the chug of the engines faltered and Jim grabbed for the doorlatch and ducked out, slammed it after.

The boat wallowed, rolled, and rock hove up starboard in the lightnings.

"I'll see if Jim needs help," Merritt said, and had his hand on the latch when *Celestine* tilted and shuddered in every plank. With a squeal of wood the boat wallowed back to rights again. Merritt let go the breath he had held and Amos breathed an obscenity.

Again the boat scraped rock and Amos put the wheel over hard in the attempt to clear it. She hung a moment, screaming, and dragged herself past the obstacle on a surge of the river.

There was no need to search after Jim: the door ripped open and he thrust his soaked head into the wheelhouse, hanging in the doorway.

"We can't get any farther, Dad, for—"

"Ain't no boat ever made farther than this, for sure," Amos shouted back. "I know son, I know, and I'm heading for the only landing we got."

He was plying the wheel with all his concentration now fixed ahead, rock walls and rocks half-submerged looking up out of the lightning-lit spray like a swift-moving nightmare. *Celestine* was moving now toward the nearside bank, where Merritt recalled a single stretch of shore that sloped gradually up to the heights beyond, a place piled high with brush and sand.

And if in seeking that shore they took *Celestine's* bottom out and the boiler blew—it would be quick, at least.

The bank entered their view, a great line of brush lit with the sporadic flashes of lightnings, between the rise and fall of *Celestine's* spray-drenched bow.

"Boy," said Amos, "you and Sam get out there on

that deck and get ready to jump. Carry cable if you can. I don't want to lose the old girl if I can help it."

Merritt grasped the doorframe and pulled himself out after Jim; and holding where they could, they worked their way to the bow and the coiled cable. The shore was coming up fast now, dipping and rising crazily in the dark, and suddenly *Celestine's* bow hit sand. The shock hurled them both to the deck, and even as they were getting to their feet again the boat was tilting and slewing round to the action of the current.

A final lightning flash showed the shore almost under them, and Jim put his hand at Merritt's back and urged him over the rail.

He hit the water, a numbing shock of cold; and for a moment he fought, then found bottom with his feet and broke surface. He moved back from *Celestine's* dark shape just as the cable snaked out and uncoiled toward his uplifted hands. Jim went over the side, and together they seized the cable and dragged it toward a projecting rock, snubbed it round and tried to hold it.

It tore from their hands, ripping flesh raw, and *Celestine* turned her bow from the shore and was taken by the current.

"*Dad!*" Jim howled into the wind.

A moment later a shadow leaped from the nearside rail into the water, a white splashing afterward in the lightnings, and Amos came stumbling up onto the bank coughing and swearing at once. He cast one look back at stricken *Celestine*, that had swung half-about and was heeling toward a swifter current, then seized Jim and Merritt each by a shoulder and turned them for the higher bank, pushing them into movement.

The scent of burning was on the wind as they came upon the road, an acrid, foul smoke. The rain had slackened by now to a spattering of drops, most of that shaken from trees by the wind, but the fire-scent was strange on the wet air.

And when they had come near the construction area itself, there was something clearly ablaze, red winking through the trees.

They kept to the woods, then, rather than venturing the open—weaponless, for all they had had gone with *Celestine*.

"Guard-post," Merritt said hoarsely, reckoning position. "Inside's dry enough to burn, once they took it."

And a moment more of moving through the dripping woods put them in clear view of it, fire-stained smoke rolling aloft into the dark. Runners of fire were licking out even to the bridge ropes, fire-dried, a lattice of flame.

There was no enemy in sight, nothing at all moving in the area of the firelight. Bodies lay in the mud in the area of the guard-station, puddles of water reflecting up fire about them.

Amos breathed an oath. Merritt cast a last look in either direction and left cover, aware that the Selbys were both with him, unasked. He scuttled to the side of a dead man, found a rifle in the mud, wiped it off, searched the man's pockets—it was one of the Burnses, Sid—and turned up two shells.

"How many men out here?" he asked of Amos, who was plundering one of the others.

"There was four this side, five the other. Looks like they got them all."

And the bridge went: burnt rope parted, and the structure swayed gracefully downward and away across the canyon, trailing burning fragments like stars.

"Sam, Dad—" Jim called suddenly, from his place nearer the rim. "There's a light moving down there."

Merritt ran to see, Amos close beside him, and they slid in beside Jim, where a large rock marked the beginning of one of the several trails down to the dam. Jim pointed. There was a faint gleam of fire far down the path, that wound down to the site, the diversion dike, from which the big flume carried its thundering load toward the black mass of the dam and over.

"Could be," said Amos, "that it's some of the boys from the farside station come down to hunt out the trouble."

"I hope it is," Merritt said, and started down.

"Sam," said Jim, catching his arm and sliding down to stop him. "You're crazy to go down there."

"What do you want? If they aren't some of ours—"

"You're going to run into more than you bargained for," said Amos. "And you're a lousy shot, Sam, leastwise with one of our kind of guns. You'd better give Jim that thing before you waste what shells we've got.—Jim, you do me a favor, son, and stay up here."

"No, sir," Jim said.

Merritt hesitated a moment; and considered Amos,

who had a rifle from one of the dead, and Jim, who had no weapon. He thrust the rifle into Jim's hands and turned and headed downhill, slipping at the turn, recovering. The two Selbys were behind him when he glanced back. He looked forward again. The lights showed, heading out away from the area of the dike. Then they went out of sight. There were some large rocks down there. He moved as rapidly as he dared, running where he could; the path was slick on the descent, clay mixed with scattered gravel. They moved, the three of them, as quickly as they could, using hands to guide them in the dark and to balance against the wind that whipped up at them from the bottom.

"I can't see it anywhere," Jim said when they reached the bottom of the trail, where was the great rush of the river on the one side of them. Merritt gasped for breath and started running the muddy and jagged ground, ran until they had reached the base of the next steps down, past the dike and down into the dark where the spillway took shape; the great timbers of the diversion flume supports rose above them, water cascading down about them in an unending shower—mere fraction of the torrent that roared overhead and thundered off the end of the flume into the pool below the dam. Sound was lost in that place; it quivered in the bones, in the brain.

Then a gleam of light showed far along that earth-work that dammed the river toward the flume, a glimmering like illusion, a trick of the eyes in the night and the curtain of water.

"There!" Merritt screamed, pointing; and close at hand a shadow moved among the supports—only that much warning, out of the tail of the eye. Merritt whirled about and caught it full in the chest, a bruising impact, bearing him backward.

A human voice shouted; that came faintly in the thunder, but he could not answer. His hands were locked at the creature's shoulders, trying to keep that face from his throat, and losing.

A shock jolted through the wiry limbs and the creature let go, staggered up with an almost-silent scream and went for Jim and Amos. Merritt came to his knees and saw another of them coming at them . . . seized up a handsized rock and lurched from knee to feet, aimed for the back of the one's head with all the power in him.

Even so it took a moment for the creature to fall—slowly, as if the hard-muscled body had a force of its own beyond the shattered brain; and in that slow moment the others closed in.

The rifles went off and hit true, dropped two of them writhing to the ground; and Merritt found himself locked with another. He avoided a first slash at his arm and hit hard enough to stagger the creature. The returned blow came low in the side, a bruising pain. He ignored that and the breathless ache that followed, smashing with dogged fury at the fanged countenance that breathed so close to his face, until the grip weakened and the lifeless body sank down, hands dragging at his clothing even as it fell.

A rifle discharged again, dim in the thunder, collapsing another of the creatures over Jim's prostrate form; and Amos bent down to heave the dead thing off his son—Jim trying weakly to get to his feet. Merritt staggered away from the support where he was leaning and started to help them, when the movement of lights still showed.

"Give me that gun," he said to Amos, trying to take the weapon, and could not—swayed on his feet when Amos jerked back on it. "They're out there by the dike," he insisted, pleading. "Amos, they're still out there."

"Stay with my boy," Amos said. "Get him out of here."

"Amos—" Merritt protested, but the elder Selby swore and pushed him roughly aside, began to run. Merritt tried to follow: the ache in his side was such that he could not run, his legs shaking under him. He brought up against one of the supports, and Amos had far outdistanced him by now. He staggered instead back to Jim, hauled him up. Jim tried to walk, tried to help him; he hastened, dragging the injured youth a limping course across the face of the dike, back again, to the base of the steps, upward.

A shot sounded feebly in the distance; and another, Merritt stopped and looked back, searching for the lights, heaved at Jim and the two of them climbed another turn of the trail, to open sky.

Another shot.

"He's still all right," Merritt.

Then incredibly there was a great flare of light, a belated shock of sound, and all that great pent-up tide crested white and poured toward the dam, washed up in one great wave and broke, crashed, thundered toward the flume supports and snapped them like kindling, boiling white at their stumps and churning over the unfinished spillway, eroding, ripping great quantities of rock away, widening the breach.

"Dad," Jim was saying, over and over again, and Merritt finally pulled him back, drew him away and up the trail, step by slow step. Sometimes he had to rest, to ease the ache in his side, and it was a long time before they reached the rim.

There he had to stop, sank to his knees and let Jim down, gasped for breath and touched at Jim's blank face.

"Jim. Jim, you hear me?"

Jim murmured something and tried to move.

"Jim, there's no place left. We've got to make it to the station, whatever' there. You understand me? They're all over these woods. Can you hold yourself up?"

For answer Jim tried to rise again, and Merritt made to help him; his hand closed on Jim's arm and Jim made an animal sound of pain, steadied himself, made drunken steps.

By now the pain in his own side had taken on a steady pulse: he was bleeding, he thought, remembered that the one who had attacked him had had a knife and did not want to feel to know. It was not a killing wound; he was still on his feet and a killing wound ought to be numb—he had heard that somewhere in his youth and chose now to believe it. He took a better grip about Jim and turned for the forest road, the way back to the station, putting from his mind what they might meet there, or how many of the People might be left.

15

"They don't close in. Why don't they close in?"

"Quiet," Merritt ordered hoarsely. He braced his weight and Jim's against the trunk of a tree, listening to the wind soughing through the branches about them. It was quiet again. It always was when they stopped to listen.

Merritt put a hand to his side and pressed, feeling dizzy. How much of what soaked his clothes was rain and how much was blood he did not want to know; but it was hard to walk any more, Jim's half-supported weight an almost intolerable burden. Jim did the best he could. His pale head jerked up as Merritt tightened his grip and he moved obedient to Merritt's direction.

The small scurrying sound was with them again. Merritt knew he might catch it by surprise if he should stop suddenly now, but it was a game he did not want to win. Their pursuers were amused, perhaps. At least for now the road was free, the station at last close at hand, up that last rise. Perhaps that was what they were waiting for; perhaps the People's sense of humor would let their quarry reach the very edge of safety; or perhaps the People were content to have destroyed the dam and were done for the night. It was no use to surmise their intentions. All that could help was to keep moving until they used their advantage for what they wanted.

The gleam of lights showed through the thinning trees now: ahead of them was the main house wall, the end of their road. Merritt heaved Jim's faltering weight a degree upward.

"Jim. Do you see? Do you see the lights? We've made it."

Jim made a sound that seemed to say he understood, and redoubled his efforts. Merritt took a better grip about him and awkwardly, by half-steps and whole, they left the wood and came along the wall, into the circle of the lights, up to the very gates of the yard.

"Who's there?" a sentry hailed them; and by those words roused men from inside, a great stirring about and shouting from inside the gates.

"Merritt and Jim Selby," Merritt shouted up. "Open up, will you? Jim is hurt. He needs help."

The gates swung inward and Merritt started forward, but armed men barred the way, rifles levelled. Merritt stared at them, knees shaking with his own weight and Jim's, and hesitated to let Jim to the ground. He thought that they might fire once Selby was clear; he was ashamed to do it, but he kept Jim upright against him.

More men were gathering, from the stockade camp outside the walls as well as from the house and the barracks. Totally surrounded, Merritt at last offered to move forward, and gave Jim into the care of two of the men from the camp. There was not a word spoken, not a sound from anyone but Jim, who moaned a protest.

And as Merritt drew back from them he chanced to look at others who had come from the main house: Hannah Burns—and Meg, Meg with her arms wrapping her coat tightly about her. She returned his stare, thin-lipped and hard of face, except that tears cast back the lantern-light.

"I tried to warn you." Merritt spoke to her, out of all of them. "I tried to stop it. No one would listen—"

"Merritt." It was Porter's voice. "Who used the explosives?"

Merritt searched among the faces, found his man as Porter came out into the light not far from him.

"Where's Amos?" Porter asked him.

"Dead," said Merritt. "Dead trying to stop them.— Why wouldn't you come? Why wouldn't you listen to me? There might have been enough of us then."

"How many are loose out there?"

"Maybe several thousand."

There was a murmuring of dismay.

"And it was you," Porter said, "it was you that stirred them up, it was your tampering with the People that brought this on, and that much you can't deny, whether you knew what you were doing or not. And for my part, I think you don't care. I think you still believe you were right, after all this."

"I had no part in it, Porter. None."

"We got kin downriver I pray to heaven got to high ground. We got farms and houses and everything we own going to be wiped out thanks to you. You've finished Hestia. You've done for us once for all. But you're not going to get on any starship this year and get away from it free. No, Sam Merritt."

"I tried to help you people," Merritt cried over the rising tide of voices. He started back as men surged toward him from the front, but there was no way of escape from the circle. Porter's men had him closed in. Meg's thin voice cried a warning, and he spun half about as they seized him from behind.

A shot rang out with a hundred yards' distance, but not from the group. As the crowd broke in terror and looked in that direction, there came a shrill scream from atop the wall just over their heads.

It was Sazhje.

"*Get it!*" Porter shouted, and a half dozen rifles turned for that target.

Merritt shouted and heaved against those holding him as the volley was fired, broke free suddenly and hurled himself at Porter, blind with rage, blind to anything but Porter's stunned face. He hit the big man twice before Porter could do more than try to fend off the blows.

Then Porter's fist slammed to his wounded side and sent the breath out of him. He staggered badly and hurled himself in again, clumsily shouldering the man to the wall, stumbling in the mud.

Something struck the back of his skull, once and again, and still he continued to hit Porter until hands tore him away and spun him aside, on hands and knees in the mud. For a moment he could not see or get his breath—but then he saw that Porter was likewise down. And the crowd—the crowd was watching something behind him.

He rose and staggered in turning, swaying on his

feet; and shook his head and wiped his eyes, blinking
things into focus. A half-dozen of the People stood at
close range, with perhaps fifty more at the forest rim;
the nearest, the tallest—had a rifle incongruously
clutched in his spidery hands.

Scurrying steps splashed across the rainsoaked
ground behind him, stopped. Merritt looked back and
saw Meg, and followed her frightened gaze to the
crest of the wall above him.

Sazhje stood there for a moment upright in the
view of all of them, then sprang to the ground, easily
absorbing the shock of that fifteen-foot drop. She
straightened and came toward him, her ears flicking
nervously, her eyes fixed on Meg with wary insolence.

"Somebody get that thing," Porter's strangled voice
shouted. "Get the Burns girl out of the way."

Meg looked back at Porter and hugged her arms
tight to her in plain refusal to move. Someone started
forward from the crowd, but stopped when no one else
moved. There was a second start forward then, several men finding their nerve at once.

"You'd better count again," Merritt shouted.
"That's just one tribe of the People standing out there,
and there's far more than what you see. They don't
look like they're going to attack unless someone
touches them off."

Another of the women from the house started to
move, and a man reached to stop her; but Hannah
Burns indignantly jerked her way free and joined her
daughter. A few of the surviving Burns men did the
same.

A man moved from the other side to join them:

George Andrews; and another: Harper, with his arm in a sling.

"Sam," said Andrews, "If you can reason with these creatures do it. We got too much to lose at it is."

Merritt put his hand on Sazhje's shoulder and she turned from facing the humans and looked up at him, her eyes all pupil.

"Ssam?" she questioned.

"Sazhje—say to Sazhje's people go, go home. Sam has enough trouble."

Her spidery arm went about him briefly, and dropped. Still she looked up at him. "Ssam ahhrht?"

"Go home, Sazhje. Sam's people might kill Sazhje. Go, go home now."

Her odd little face contracted in an expression of distress. She touched his hurt, frowned up at him. Ears flicked. "Sazhje people no make kill tam. Wa come, Ssam. Ssam people kill. Ssam come Sazhje people, go 'igh, 'igh."

He caressed her silk-smooth cheek, shook his head. "No, Sazje. Sam can't. Sam can't come. Sam's people are here, this place, Sam's place."

"Ssam stay?"

"Yes. Go on, go on, Sazhje. Go home while you can."

She stepped back from him and started away, looked back once as she was crossing the ground between and once as she had nearly rejoined her own. Then she stopped . . . in a visible agony of decision, slammed her fists against her thighs and screamed something at one of her kind who held the rifle: Otrekh, surely Otrekh. Her voice pleaded, scolded, so impassioned an oration that there was no stir from either side.

"Sam," said Andrews from close on Merritt's left. "Can you understand any of that?"

Merritt shook his head. "I can talk to her in our language, but not in hers. She said she thought the flood would come on us soon. She doesn't think we have much of a chance."

"Why did you go to them?"

"Are you only now asking that?" Merritt returned, and did not bother to answer; it was too much effort.

Otrekh cut off Sazhje's appeal with a brusque move of the rifle he held; and she hesitated, then ran anxiously back to the very edge of the human group, stopped, leaned forward and shouted.

"Otrekh say no make kill Ssam people. Ssam people ahhrht, Ssam. Ah! Sazhje people no kill. No make tam, no tam—Sazhje people ahhrht. Ssam people go 'igh, ah, ah, Ssam! Sazhje come 'morrow. Sazhje make ahhrht Ssam people. Ssam-Zhim-Ssam people come 'morrow 'igh, 'igh."

"Can you understand that?" Andrews asked him. "Is that human talk she's using now?"

Merritt nodded, looked back at the others. "She says," he shouted in his strained voice, "that it wasn't her tribe that blew up the dam, that she's talked with the head man and he's willing to let humans into the uplands if there's no dam. They know we're desperate. And this time you'd better listen."

"They'll massacre us," someone shouted.

"Then stay in the lowlands and drown! No one can help you then. This is the only chance you have."

"No," someone else cried, and Merritt saw Porter snatch a rifle from a man near him—he shouted a warning to Sazhje in the same instant that others moved, struck the rifle up. It discharged helplessly into the air and several men combined to wrench it from Porter's grasp. One of them was one of the Miller boys, who came up with the rifle.

"We've had a bellyfull of advice that's lost us lives and lost us the dam. We haven't got any more to lose, Sam. Is that creature telling the truth?"

"To the best I know, she is," Merritt answered, "and it's the best and only thing we've got. We'll go out in the valley, we'll gather families here at the station, behind walls; and with them safe, some of us can trust ourselves to the People's word and go into the high hills. The station rock will hold, whatever comes downriver, and we'll build again where it's suitable to them and us. We aren't done yet."

"He's right," said one of the Burns men. "It's by far the best we've got. Get cleared away behind walls, the lot of you, and we'll sort this out when we've got things settled down again, by daylight."

Men began to mill backward, slowly, mistrustfully—but some of the men with Andrews still remained.

"George," said Merritt, "go on, get the rest of them out of here. And keep an eye on Porter."

"Will you be all right out here?"

Merritt nodded, waited, holding his side, until Andrews and all the rest had gone. There was Sazhje, still standing and waiting for his answer. He held out his hand to her and she came to take it.

"It's all right. Sazhje, when the water comes, men's places will go. We'll need food, understand—food, food. Many Sam's people come here, stay— understand?"

"Ah," said Sazhje. "Sazhje say Otrekh."

"Otrekh won't kill the people."

"No kill, Ssam. Otrekh say no kill." Her slim strange hands pressed on his. "Ssam come Sazhje. Come Sazhje."

He shook his head sadly. "That's not going to work at all, Sazhje. No—no, Sam can't, can't stay with Sazhje."

She seemed to have expected that answer. She glanced past at something behind him and then up into his face very sadly. Her hands slipped from his and then she moved off quickly to join Otrekh and the others. Once more she looked back.

"Ssam," she said as an afterthought. "Gairh kill tam—tam kill Gairh, Gairh people. No Gairh." And her face broke into a satisfied smile. With a swinging, cheerful step she crossed the final distance and joined her people in their retreat.

Merritt watched them go, and then feeling the misery of his injuries once more, he turned with a careful move and started for the gate, stopped again as he saw Meg standing in his path.

She waited for him and took his arm as they entered the yard. "Come on," she said gently. "Come on, Sam."

16

Merritt looked the papers over, glanced across the
table at the governor's desk, signed them one after
the other, passed them to Lee under the witness of
the silver-suited officer from *Pilgrim*. The governor
signed; the officer affixed his own signature, gathered
up the papers.

"A formality," Merritt said. "There'll be a man on
Pele, or somewhere along the way; went out on *Adam
Jones*. Don't know if the money will ever catch up to
him; but it's his if he wants his half. Mine's to the
account of the colony."

The officer looked uncomfortable, regarded the governor, and the silver-suited men who had come with
him stood by the door, unmoving through the entire
exchange.

Merritt read the looks; they were not that difficult.
"I'll walk you downstairs," he said. "The governor
won't object. My business here is finished."

"The contract is settled," the governor said, offering
an anxious look, a conciliatory gesture. "It's quit, so
far as we're concerned."

The officer from *Pilgrim* looked him up and down,
signalled his men, who opened the door. Merritt

213

walked with them, hands in pockets; the door closed after them as they started down the unpainted board stairs.

"We'll get you out of here," the man from the ships said. "We've leave to do it, and the weapons. Don't refuse from fear of losing. We have the beacon-message. That's on file. Whatever force we need— we'll break this colony up if we have to."

Merritt shook his head. "You've got the papers with you. See my partners up ahead somewhere, that's all." He opened the unpainted door, walked out with them into the rain, his own homespun absorbing what their silver shed. He offered his hand. "Goodbye, sir. And thanks. I'll hope you have those supplies set off. A wagon will move them. We're going to appreciate the help we get in that regard. It's been short, this year."

"You're sure. No help needed."

"I'm sure." He pocketed his hand again, turned from them, walked up the street past the open shops. The silver shape of the starship shuttle showed over the brown roofs. It was festival . . . a subdued one, for *Pilgrim* had sent her shuttle down armed; but things would begin to ease: there would be new Hestians come summer.

He walked up the street to the town's edge, to the dockside, down the wooden steps, and up to one of the two boats that rode at moorings there. She had a great deal of new wood in her hull, did *Celestine*, but salvage was a way of life in the backriver.

His steps aboard roused Jim out; the young river-man stirred out of the wheelhouse and gave him a look up and down as if looking for some sign of outsider about him.

"Going to have cargo this trip," Merritt said, looked anxiously up as Meg too exited the wheelhouse and crossed the deck to him. She put her arms about him; he smoothed her hair, wondering what things she had wondered, if she had expected him back.

"Hear there's guns in town," Jim said.

Merritt shrugged. "They'll settle. They'll settle. Shuttle will set the supplies off and clear that beacon with the ship so there's no trouble with the next landing. We'll be on our way in the morning."

"Now," Meg said. And with a sharp look at the town and all the sweep of it, the ship and the lagoon: "Jim, there's *Hazel* here to freight those supplies upriver. Let's get out of here. Now. This minute."

Jim hesitated. Merritt started to object the senselessness of it; but of a sudden Jim nodded emphatically. "Right," he said. "Got our own business."

And he strode back to the engine, and soon enough there was life from it, a slow thumping, the while he ran to shout orders to men lounding ashore. Cables were cast off; Merritt seized up the bow cable to haul it in, coiled it dripping on the deck, the while Jim hauled the other in and ran for the wheel.

Celestine steadied, headed out into the channel with assurance. The town fell astern. The cold autumn wind and the persistent mist made it cold on deck, and Merritt hugged Meg close to him, walked into the lee of the wheelhouse.

The brown water curled away under them, and reed-rimmed banks, heaped with the trunks of trees,

passed slowly by. On the second day they saw a fisher
plying the river, a curious figure all tucked up and
leaning over on the bank. It looked up as they passed,
made a little turning of its head . . . naked and down-
covered, one of the People, grown uncommonly bold
for so far downriver.

It had a fish. It clutched its prize anxiously, rose to
watch them as they went.

There was the bright scar of a road on the height,
that came down from the new settlement, and went
both ways along the southside. It would reach New
Hope by summer.

And there were ruins, houses that were deserted
now, fields that stood reed-grown, hazed in the persistent mist.

On the third day, at dawn, the shuttle would have
lifted. Merritt stood at the rail, looking at the sky in
that quarter, which was hazed and clouded . . .
shrugged finally and turned away, to find Meg pre-
tending she had not seen him look; he came and
slipped his arm in hers.

"I don't miss it," he said, and looked up at the banks
ahead of them, familiar territory. They had sight of
the hills now, that began materializing out of the
rain-haze.

"Sam," Jim called at him. "Easy steering here.
Want to have a turn at the wheel? I'll trust you. I'm
for a nap and keeping going tonight: station by
tomorrow suppertime."

He climbed the steps up and went inside, Meg
behind him, took the steering into his hands as Jim
gave Meg a nod and closed the door in leaving. Meg

settled on the sill that rimmed the wheelhouse, rose finally to stand beside him and watch the river.

"Going up to the new settlement when the supplies come in," he said to her. "I think we can at least get the station road finished this winter."

"I'm coming," she said.

He looked down at her, took her at her word . . . gave his attention to the river again, feeling the currents.

"Sam?" she said.

"They looked different," he said, "the ones from the ship. There was nothing about them I recognized." He indicated ahead, where the hills showed graygreen through the rain. "I didn't talk about that—Upriver. None of their concern . . . yet. When Hestians meet the ships on their own terms . . . so will the Upriver. That's best, I think."

"Children's children, before that happens."

He nodded, reckoning it so. Meg leaned on the sill forward, hair misted with rain, wiped the moisture from her face. In the hills autumn colors showed, oranges and bluegreens and browns, deepening into twilight haze, and finally into dark.

But there were no lights along the river this year, none, until the station.

C. J. CHERRYH

"C. J. Cherryh just keeps getting better and better" –
Marion Zimmer Bradley

Angel with the Sword

From the moment Altair Jones hauls Mondragon into her barge she becomes entangled in a deadly power game. Fine-boned and fair, the mysterious Mondragon looks like a high-born from the fabulous upper levels; certainly he will not survive long in the putrid underworld of the canal folk.

Against all her instincts, Altair determines to conceal him from the assassins and fanatics who threaten his life. But unless she can learn the truth about Mondragon, there is nothing her extraordinary cunning or her ferocious love can do to protect him.

"A rare treat . . . Cherryh is in top form" –
Roger Zelazny

C. J. CHERRYH

"The most versatile talent of the 80s" –
New York Times

The Dreamstone

The days of Magic were dying, the era of Man had
dawned. Yet in one small place the Faery power
prevailed, in one quiet wood its bright force shone still.
In the forest of Ealdwood dwelt one with more
patience, more pride and more love of the earth than
any other being in that troubled world. In the depths of
Ealdwood dwelt Arafel, the last defender of Faery
against the trespass of Mankind!

The Tree of Swords and Jewels

They said he had the cast of magic on him, that elvish
blood ran in his veins and that he knew that other world
where Arafel, the last of the Daoine Sidhe, held sway.
But what had been a blessing was now a curse, for envy
of Ciaran Cuilean grew deep in the hearts of men . . .

ANDRE NORTON

The Witch World Series

"Rich, brilliant, superbly imaginative" – Lin Carter

Witch World

The moment he pledged himself to the defence of Estcarp, Simon Tregarth, fugitive from Earth, embarked on a journey of magic and peril from which there was no return.

Web of the Witch World

Simon Tregarth and his witch-wife Jaelithe knew there could be no peace until they tracked Estcarp's enemy to its lair – and smashed the Gateway to its world. But what if their only chance was for Tregarth to offer up his mind to the monstrous power of Kolder?

Year of the Unicorn

They were paying the price of an unholy alliance, forged against the dread hounds of Alizon. But were not those thirteen maidens too high a price to pay?

ANDRE NORTON

"If the *Witch World* had never been written, so many
other worlds would be the poorer" –
C. J. Cherryh

Three Against the Witch World

For the sons of Simon Tregarth, the only hope was
exile. So to the East they turned, to a country whose
skill and sorcery the Wise Ones had for centuries
sought to hide.

Warlock of the Witch World

Enemies human and monstrous, weapons of magic and
stealth ... all must fall before warrior, warlock and
sorceress can reunite against the power of doom.

Sorceress of the Witch World

At the very heart of evil lay hope ... if only the broken
sorceress could summon the power to seek it out.

TITLES AVAILABLE FROM
VGSF

The prices shown below were correct at the time
of going to press (December 1987)

☐ 03995 7	WITCH WORLD	Andre Norton	£2.50
☐ 03990 6	THE MASKS OF TIME	Robert Silverberg	£2.95
☐ 04008 4	HEGIRA	Greg Bear	£2.95
☐ 04032 7	THE FACELESS MAN	Jack Vance	£2.50
☐ 03987 6	NIGHT WALK	Bob Shaw	£2.50
☐ 04009 2	ANGEL WITH THE SWORD	C.J. Cherryh	£2.95
☐ 04022 X	MISSION OF GRAVITY	Hal Clement	£2.50
☐ 03988 4	THE OTHER SIDE OF THE SKY		
		Arthur C. Clarke	£2.95
☐ 03996 5	WEB OF THE WITCH WORLD	Andre Norton	£2.50
☐ 04010 6	EYE AMONG THE BLIND	Robert Holdstock	£2.50
☐ 04007 6	STAR GATE	Andre Norton	£2.50
☐ 03989 2	TO LIVE AGAIN	Robert Silverberg	£2.95
☐ 03999 X	YEAR OF THE UNICORN	Andre Norton	£2.50
☐ 04053 X	THE BRAVE FREE MEN	Jack Vance	£2.50
☐ 04096 3	MEDUSA'S CHILDREN	Bob Shaw	£2.50
☐ 04011 4	EARTHWIND	Robert Holdstock	£2.95
☐ 03998 1	THREE AGAINST THE WITCH WORLD		
		Andre Norton	£2.50
☐ 04044 0	THE DREAMSTONE	C.J. Cherryh	£2.50
☐ 04124 2	STAR MAN'S SON	Andre Norton	£2.50
☐ 04038 6	UP THE LINE	Robert Silverberg	£2.95
☐ 04125 0	QUEST OF THE THREE WORLDS		
		Cordwainer Smith	£2.50
☐ 04052 1	THE ASUTRA	Jack Vance	£2.50
☐ 03997 3	WARLOCK OF THE WITCH WORLD		
		Andre Norton	£2.50

Also available: VGSF CLASSICS

☐ 03819 5	THE SIRENS OF TITAN	Kurt Vonnegut	£3.50
☐ 03821 7	MORE THAN HUMAN	Theodore Sturgeon	£3.50
☐ 03820 9	A TIME OF CHANGES	Robert Silverberg	£3.50
☐ 03818 7	NOVA	Samuel R. Delany	£3.50
☐ 03849 7	THE CITY AND THE STARS	Arthur C. Clarke	£3.50

Continued overleaf

All these books are available at your shop or newsagent or can be ordered direct from the publisher. Just tick the titles you want and fill in the form below.

VGSF, Cash Sales Department, PO Box 11, Falmouth, Cornwall.

Please send cheque or postal order, no currency.

Please allow cost of book(s) plus the following for postage and packing:

UK customers – Allow 60p for the first book, 25p for the second book plus 15p for each additional book ordered, to a maximum charge of £1.90.

BFPO – Allow 60p for the first book, 25p for the second book plus 15p per copy for the next seven books, thereafter 9p per book.

Overseas customers including Eire – Allow £1.25 for the first book, 75p for the second book plus 28p for each additional book ordered.

NAME (Block letters) ....

ADDRESS ....

....

....